D1553195

Home
to the
Mountains

A Fawn for Christmas

A novel by

William Delia

ISBN: 9781515068945 (softcover)

Printed in the United States of America

DEDICATION

Home can be an elusive thing, yet I have been blessed to discover as an adult the home that I longed for all my life. To my wife Regina and our entire family I dedicate not only this book, but my life and my unconditional love

Prologue

The doe stood motionless, almost invisible in the dense underbrush, as she silently nibbled on a slender alder branch. Her ears pricked forward and her eyes twitched from side to side alert to any unfamiliar sound or movement. Satisfied with the stillness, she lowered her head and nuzzled the November snow at her feet. Today the snow lightly covered the ground, but she knew that soon it would shroud the trees and bury the land making food, even alder branches, hard to find.

Instinctively, she sensed something was not right; her belly was heavy, swollen with new life. She knew that her fawn should come in the warm days of spring, but this fawn would not wait; it would be born in the bitter cold of the winter that lay ahead.

She moved on, her rounded underbelly swaying from side-to-side; walking more unsteadily with each passing day. Now she seldom strayed more than a few hundred yards from the ancient spruce tree whose low-hanging limbs sheltered her from the cold. After one final furtive glance at the woods around her, she slipped beneath the branches and eased herself to the ground. Weary and worn she rested her head on her forelegs and slept.

Book I – Deer Run

I'm goin' home to the mountains
Goin' back from where I came
I've been so lost and forgotten
I don't remember the sound
Of my own name

-   *Home to the Mountains*
    © William Delia

Chapter One

Rafford Brown walked up the path from the river in the last light of a mid-November day. He passed through a sparse stand of evergreens, circled around a small, empty livestock pen and approached the two-story white clapboard farmhouse. He paused for a moment to watch the sun disappear behind Hart Mountain and then continued up the porch steps to the front door. Rafford took off his battered suede fedora and ran his fingers through his shaggy brown hair, hoping to look a bit more presentable. As he reached out to knock on the door, a dog inside the house began barking loud enough to shake the dust from the doorjamb.

A woman's voice shouted, "Smokey! Quiet down!"

The door opened a crack and an elderly woman peered out. At first glance, she appeared small and frail, but something in her eyes conveyed a gentle strength.

"Good evening, ma'am," Rafford said with a smile. "That's quite a doorbell you've got there."

"Good evening," she said as she eyed the stranger.

"I'm sorry to disturb you, but I am paddling down river from Colvin Lake and I need a place to camp for the night. Would it be all right if I slept in the woods, down by the river?"

She hesitated before asking, "So you'll be portaging into Deer Pond then on down to the Sacandaga River?"

"Actually, I planned to carry into Elm Lake," Rafford smiled again, knowing she was testing his story. "I'm sorry to bother you so late; I thought I could make the portage tonight and camp on state land further downstream. I guess I was a bit overconfident."

"I don't normally allow people to camp; Deer Run is all posted land, you know."

"Yes, ma'am, I saw the signs along the river."

"I suppose it'll be all right. But just one night," she said firmly, "and be careful with your fire; it's been very dry this year."

"Thank you. I will be careful," he said as he stepped down from the porch. "I'll be on my way early in the morning, so I won't disturb you anymore. Thanks, again."

As he walked away, she called after him, "If you'd like, you can have a hot breakfast with the hired hands before you leave. They eat here on the porch at seven a.m."

"Thank you, ma'am, that's very kind. I guess I'll see you in the morning."

Rafford walked back across the driveway, past the barn and into the woods. On his way down to the river, he gathered an armload of twigs and branches and two ragged squares of birch bark. He pitched his tent in a small clearing overlooking the river. A few stones from the river's edge made a serviceable fire ring where he quickly ignited a small stack of dry branches using flaming strips of birch bark. As the fire settled into glowing coals, he divided the last of his beans and pemmican jerky into two portions; he put one on to cook and carefully stored the other for one more meal. While the beans cooked, he took out his map and counted the miles to Normantown.

"Two days," he said aloud, "if I don't lose too much time on the portages."

When he had eaten, he stirred down the coals, doused the fire, and then took three warm stones from the fire ring into the tent. It would be a cold night, even for November. He lay in his sleeping bag, reading and listened to the familiar sounds of night in the Adirondacks. The steady chatter of the river rattling over its stony bed droned beneath the whisper of the evening breeze in the pines. From a distance, the call of a loon swirled through the dark. Rafford closed his eyes and felt the peace of the river embrace him as he drifted away. His last thought before sleep was to wonder if the dream would come again this night.

Morning dawned cold and damp with a heavy frost covering the ground. Rafford broke camp quickly following his well-practiced routine. He loaded his backpack and then tied the rolled-up sleeping bag and pad to the bottom of the pack frame. He wiped the frost and condensation from the small A-frame tent and packed it carefully before strapping the rolled tent to the top of his backpack. His breath billowed in white puffs around his head as he worked, a reminder that winter was close-at-hand. When his gear was neatly stored beneath the overturned canoe, he started up the path to the house.

Everything about the place appeared smaller and more crowded in the bright light of morning. The barn, two adjacent outbuildings and a livestock pen framed one side of the open barnyard. The sound of bleating goats in the pen echoed off the barn walls. Chickens wandered freely and a few perched on an old Kubota tractor in the barn that, judging by the dust and the poultry, had not moved in some time. A hand-carved wooden sign, *Deer Run*, hung over the open barn door. The sturdy white farmhouse on the opposite side of the barnyard shone brightly in the early morning sun. Rafford noticed that all of the structures appeared solidly built, but all were showing their age.

He walked toward the house as he heard the woman call out, "Breakfast is ready!"

"Good morning, ma'am."

"Good morning. Come sit down while it's hot. This young fellow is Johnny Paige; he and his brothers work for me. I'm sorry I don't know your name, Mr. -", her voice trailed away.

"Brown. Rafford Brown."

The woman extended her hand to him, "I'm Abigail Sherwood, Mr. Brown, and this is Smokey," she said pointing to the large dusty-brown Labrador who shadowed the woman's every move.

The three of them sat at a table on the porch laden with hot biscuits, scrambled eggs and a platter of thick sliced ham steaks. The aroma filled Rafford's nostrils making his mouth water and his stomach rumble loud enough to be heard over the sounds of the goats and the chickens in the barnyard. The woman passed the platters of food and although Rafford tried not to overload his plate, he smiled sheepishly when his second piece of ham pushed one of his biscuits off onto the table. He was famished and ready to dig in when he noticed the woman and the boy bow their heads.

"We thank you, O Lord, for the gift of this day, for your presence that surrounds us and for this meal that will fill us. We thank you, too, for Mr. Brown who shares this meal with us and we pray your healing touch upon the Paige boys. We pray all of this in your name. Amen."

They ate breakfast with little conversation. Rafford thought to himself that Johnny Paige looked to be no more than fifteen years old. He wondered about Johnny's brothers; two other places were set at the table, but no one else arrived.

When they had finished eating and the woman took the dishes inside, the boy spoke, "You just passing through?"

Rafford nodded, "On my way to Normantown."

"Good. She's a nice old lady, but you wouldn't want to stay here long. There's nothing 'round here 'cept a few scrawny farm animals and a scraggly bunch of freeloading deer."

The woman returned with a brown paper sack for each of them. "Johnny, when you leave today, take these muffins home to your brothers. I hope they get well soon; there is a lot to do before winter sets in."

"Mrs. Sherwood, I, uh," the boy stammered and looked at the ground, then he took a deep breath and blurted out, "they ain't really sick. They just don't want to work here no more."

"Oh, I see," the woman replied. "Well, I guess that means you and I will have to work even harder. I'm glad you –"

"I can't work here anymore either, after today," the boy interrupted. "I'm sorry, Mrs. Sherwood."

She sat down at the table and took a long drink of her coffee. The boy squirmed in the silence for several moments then jumped to his feet.

"I'll go milk the goats," he said as he headed off toward the barn.

Rafford nursed his coffee and studied the woman. He guessed she was in her sixties, and apparently lived here alone. He liked her confident way and thought to himself that, on a good day, she could probably outwork Johnny Paige and his brothers combined. Still, preparing for winter in the mountains was no easy chore.

Rafford cleared his throat, and when she turned toward him, he spoke, "Mrs. Sherwood, you've been kind to me; perhaps I can repay you with a good day's work. If you don't mind me camping in your woods another night, I'd be happy to work with Johnny for the day."

The woman studied him for a moment and then smiled, "That's very kind of you, Mr. Brown. If you can spare the time, we have plenty to do, but I will pay you for your trouble, just as I would have paid the Paige brothers. Johnny will show you what needs to be done."

Rafford worked as hard that day as any day he could remember. He and the boy spent the morning in the barn, first tending the goats and chickens and then moving bales of hay from the back of the barn to dry storage in the loft. At least, the loft was supposed to be dry; with several large holes in the old shake roof, the hayloft was far from watertight.

At midday, Mrs. Sherwood called them back to the house for more of her home cooking: sausages, fried potatoes, fresh vegetables and more homemade biscuits. Every bite was a treat to Rafford, after days of eating beans and not much else. As soon as they had finished lunch, they went right back to work. They passed the entire afternoon moving firewood from a clearing behind the barn to the side of the house. Loading, carting, unloading and stacking each piece was hard, tedious work. Johnny worked well for a boy, but that was to be expected from someone who has grown up in the mountains. By the time the sun went down, they had created an impressive woodpile, but Rafford knew it would dwindle quickly in the coming winter.

The woman met them on the porch with a pay envelope for each of them. The boy took his money with a somewhat guilty look, and hastily disappeared down the driveway. Rafford tried to refuse, but the woman would hear none of it.

"Dinner will be ready in 20 minutes. You can wash up in the barn."

Abigail produced a delicious meal of chicken and dumplings followed by hot apple pie served with slabs of the sharpest white cheddar Rafford had ever tasted. He hemmed and hawed when Abigail asked him to say grace, until she once again offered a simple prayer of thanks. He was not used to this – three delicious meals, and three prayers, in one day. He relished the home cooking but prayer had not been a part of his life for a long time.

They ate in the kitchen, and although they spoke sparingly, each seemed to enjoy the other's company. After dinner, Rafford washed the dishes while Abigail dried and kept up polite conversation. Finally, the talk got around to the subject the evening's conversation had danced around but not spoken aloud.

Rafford spoke first, "Mrs. Sherwood, we worked hard today, but there is still a lot to do before winter. The holes in the hay loft roof should be patched, the siding on the north side of the house needs work, and the firewood we stacked today will likely be gone before Christmas."

"This is a big old place, Mr. Brown; I know I have a lot to do. What is your point?"

"I don't truly have a point, Mrs. Sherwood, but if you want, I could stay on a few more days and maybe get some of these things done."

The woman looked at him for several moments before answering, "That's very kind, but I don't want to keep you from completing your trip. Don't you have to be somewhere, downriver?"

"I'm on my way to Normantown to work for the winter. But a few more days won't hurt."

"Mr. Brown –"

"Please call me Rafford," he interjected.

"Fine, Rafford, it's none of my business, but I can't help but wonder. Are you on vacation or . . ." the woman's voice trailed off.

"I guess you could call it an extended vacation. I've been canoeing and camping in the Adirondacks for nearly two years, working odd jobs when my supplies run low. It's been great, but the winter months are tough. Last year, I camped through December, but in mid-January, I gave in to the cold and passed the rest of the winter in Tupper Lake Village. This year I thought I would give Normantown a try."

"You mean you have been living in a tent for two years?" she stammered. "What about your family, a career? You can't be much more than thirty years old; you're obviously bright, well-educated, don't you have things to do with your life?"

"I'm thirty-four and, with all due respect Mrs. Sherwood, I am doing something with my life; I'm living it," Rafford's voice had an unintended edge.

"I'm sorry I pried, Mr. Brown. It's none of my business."

"No need to apologize; I'm not easily offended."

For a while, they sat in silence, then Abigail said in a gentle voice, "If you are still willing to stay, I could use your help, Mr. Brown. I'll pay you a fair wage, and there's a bunk in the tack room where you can sleep."

"That will be fine, Mrs. Sherwood. If you will list the jobs you want done, I'll get started first thing in the morning."

The tack room provided Spartan accommodations, but to Rafford it felt like pure luxury. He laid a fire in the cast-iron Franklin stove, and soon the room glowed in the warm flickering light of the flames.

He lay on the bunk and thought about this place and how he came to be here. It seemed almost too coincidental, as if maybe he was here for a reason. Ever since he had first come to the Adirondacks, as a boy, he had dreamed about a home like this one. Nothing fancy, just a house, a barn, some land and a few animals; a peaceful place surrounded by the beauty of the mountains. Over the past two years, he had seen such places many times from a distance, but they always seemed elusive and far beyond his reach. Now here he was at Deer Run, where Abigail Sherwood was living the life he longed for. Knowing that someone else had found it encouraged him to think perhaps one day he might find it, too.

Rafford rolled over and reached for his backpack. From the front pocket, he pulled a worn leather-bound Bible, opened it and took out the photograph tucked inside the front cover. Angling the picture toward the flickering light from the wood stove, he felt an aching emptiness wash over him. Still, he had to smile when he looked at the face in the worn photo. It seemed a lifetime ago but he could still remember every detail about her. He especially remembered her smile – a smile that always seemed to be just for him.

The light from the fire began to fade and he carefully replaced the picture in the Bible and secured the book in his pack. He lay back, closed his eyes and let the memories carry him; memories of a different place and time, far away, where promises were kept and where love lasted forever.

Somewhere along the way, he slept.

ॐॐ
Chapter Two

A bigail Sherwood lingered in the kitchen long after Rafford had gone to move his things into the tack room. She thought about their conversation and wondered what kind of man leaves everything behind and treks off into the mountains? A smile crossed her face when she realized she knew exactly the kind of man who would do such a thing. She had followed a man like that to the Adirondacks more than 40 years ago.

Rafford Brown and her late husband Roger Sherwood probably had much in common, she thought, and though separated by many years, they likely would have been good friends. She wondered if it was divine providence that Rafford, so much like Roger, should arrive here at the very moment when Abigail felt most alone and most in need of help.

She met Roger Sherwood when they were both teenagers. Abigail and her mother had moved to Gloversville, New York in 1946. Her father had been killed in the fighting on Iwo Jima, leaving them no choice but to move in with her Aunt Shirley, herself a war-widow. Shirley had a good job in one of the many leather tanneries that earned Gloversville the title of "Glove City". Her mother quickly found work as a housekeeper for one of the tannery owners, and Abigail enrolled at Gloversville High for her senior year.

Abigail Simmons and Roger Sherwood and were brought together more by the alphabet than anything else. They had little in common, beyond last names that began with the letter "S". She had grown-up in the city – in near-by Schenectady – where, before the war, her father had struggled to support his family by working as an unskilled laborer at General Electric. Roger's family was wealthy, by comparison, living well by logging thousands of acres of Adirondack forest they owned or for which they leased logging rights. Roger would be the first of his family to graduate from high school, and the family had high expectations for him. Abigail knew her family had no aspirations at all, for her. She was bright and not very attractive so, in their view, her prospects were limited. She knew her mother secretly hoped a man returning from the war would be willing to overlook her plainness, marry Abigail and provide for them both.

Abigail and Roger would probably not have noticed one another if not for their school's compulsion about seating students in alphabetical order. As a result, they sat next to one another day after day, in class after class, and ended up becoming good friends. They never dated each other, or anyone else for that matter. When they said farewell at graduation, they did not expect to see one another again.

Jobs were scarce in 1947 and war veterans were given preference for any position that became available. Aunt Shirley managed to find a part-time job for Abigail at the tannery, filling in when the regulars were out sick. She hated the tannery work, especially the smell from the hides and the chemicals used to treat them, but her mother's health had deteriorated and they depended upon the little money she earned.

Abigail dated infrequently in spite of the combined recruiting efforts of Aunt Shirley and her mother. The crude men from the tannery spent their free time either drunk or well on their way to getting drunk. She managed to avoid them, and their unwelcome pursuit, by spending her free time either in church or exploring the near-by mountains.

At church, she sang in the choir, volunteered with the ladies mission society, and led two Bible study groups. Her mother nagged her about spending so much time with church women saying she would never find a husband there, but secretly she envied her daughter's faith; a faith she had never found herself.

When not at church, Abigail spent every free moment in the mountains. She joined the Adirondack Mountain Club and passed her days-off hiking the nearby mountain trails. She was captivated by the tranquility of the forest, and the beauty of rivers, streams and lakes too numerous to count.

One Saturday afternoon, as she hiked a favorite trail along the banks of the Jessup River, she spotted something unusual in the water. Squinting her eyes against the bright sunlight, she saw the motionless body of a deer lying on the edge of the gravel bar that divided the river. The doe lay on her side, partly submerged in the swiftly flowing water. An empty sadness flowed over Abigail. She had seen hunters driving through town with their trophy bucks strapped to their cars for all to admire, but she never understood their sense of pride. Stalking and killing something as defenseless and peaceful as a deer made no sense to her, even though she understood that hunting was part of mountain life. However, hunting season had ended months ago and yet here was a deer left to die in the river. She was certain that if she were closer she would see the fatal bullet hole stained with red.

Suddenly, something moved on the opposite bank of the river. A tiny fawn lay on the muddy edge of the Jessup looking completely helpless. She guessed it was no more than a few days old and she knew it was unlikely to survive motherless and on its own. She dropped her day pack, stepped out of her boots and then stripped down to her skivvies and waded into the river. The water only reached her waist at its deepest spot, and even though the current was strong, she quickly reached the opposite bank.

The fawn made no effort to escape. It lay perfectly still, except for the rapid twitching of its two enormous brown eyes that tracked her every movement. She slowly reached out and began to stroke the fawn's neck. The animal trembled at her touch – cold or fear, she wondered? Then she notice she was trembling, too, chilled by her wet clothes and the late afternoon breeze.

Still not sure what she would do, she scooped up the fawn in one smooth motion. Its long legs dangled awkwardly, but she was surprised by how little it weighed. She clutched the animal tight to her chest and waded back into the river, thinking about her dry clothes and trying to remember what she had packed in her rucksack. She stepped carefully, leaning her weight against the current, struggling to keep her balance. She glanced up-river and spotted a canoe coming towards her. The lone man in the canoe appeared to hold a rifle in one hand – the hunter! She was almost to the midpoint of the river, no time to turn back, so she quickened her steps. The man in the canoe picked up the pace, paddling hard now, closing the gap between them. He wants the fawn, she thought! Her legs felt impossibly heavy as she pushed through the water, moving as though she were walking in slow motion. The canoe was closing fast when she felt the river bottom begin angling upward toward the shore. Just a few more steps and they would be safely on the riverbank. Her very next step, however, landed on a rock worn smooth by the constant movement of the river and slickened by a thin coat of algae. As soon as she felt the rock under her foot, she knew she was lost. She leaned upstream but her foot slid downstream and both she and the fawn fell back into the river, with only her head staying above the water.

She struggled back to her knees still clutching the fawn to her chest; both of them startled and soaked, but unhurt. As she tried to stand, she heard the canoe scrape to a halt on the riverbank between her and safety.

"Are you alright?" said the man in the canoe.

"Stay away from me!" she shrieked, with a little more drama than she intended.

"Here, let me help you with that fawn," he offered.

"You've already killed one deer today, isn't that enough?" she replied angrily.

"What in blue blazes are you talking about? I'm just trying to help – you will never get to your feet in that current unless you let go of the deer. Let me take the fawn."

She knew he was right, but she was afraid of what he would do. Still, she had no choice; she and the fawn were shaking uncontrollably in the icy cold water. The man stepped out of the canoe and waded toward her just enough to take the fawn from her outstretched arms. She struggled to her feet and followed him to the riverbank.

He quickly tied the fawn to the painter line on the bow of his canoe. Then he turned toward Abigail, looking her over, up and down.

"You must be freezing," he said as he took off his woolen shirt and offered it to her.

"I have dry clothes over there" she replied.

"Well I figured you wouldn't be out here dressed like that," he said with a half-smile.

She suddenly realized that she was standing there in soaking wet underwear that clung to every bump on her body. What was not easily seen certainly would be easily imagined. Her modesty gone, she decided to retain what little dignity she had left by not giving him the satisfaction of seeing her embarrassment.

Before she could think of the right thing to say, he turned away and said, "I'll get a fire started while you change."

In a few minutes, they were sitting by a small fire. She was still chilled and shivering, but she wore dry clothes. The man was using his wool shirt to dry the trembling fawn.

He glanced toward the river where the doe lay, "Looks like this one's on his own, now. He won't stand much of a chance out here."

"Well, you should have thought of that before you shot his mother – and out of season, I might add," she snapped.

"Is that what you think? Well, first of all, this is private land and I can do whatever I choose on my own property. But just to set the record straight, I didn't shoot Bambi's mother."

"You can't lie to me; I saw your rifle as you came around the bend."

"Oh, you did?" He got up and walked to the canoe. He picked up a fishing rod and pointed it at her. "Well that explains why I didn't catch any fish with this thing – imagine, I thought it was a fly rod, and all along it was a hunting rifle!"

He was clearly enjoying himself now. "But, then, you always were smarter than me, Abigail Simmons."

The sound of his laughter took her straight back to high school, "Roger Sherwood."

"Hello, Abigail"

"Why didn't you say something?"

"I was too busy defending my motives for trying to help a lady in distress. Besides, I wasn't sure it was you, at first. But then I realized nobody could do righteous indignation like you," he said with a teasing smile.

They sat by the fire awhile getting reacquainted. Roger told her how he had gone to Paul Smiths College to study forestry and then come home to manage the family logging business. His father, however, did not agree with his modern theories about renewable forests and conservation. Their family had always clear-cut – it produced more lumber, cheaper and quicker – and that was what his father would continue to do. The two of them had argued constantly, until

Roger had finally walked out. Years earlier, Roger's father had deeded five hundred acres of timber to each of the children for tax purposes. When Roger walked out, he moved onto his five hundred acres and built a cabin. Then, just to anger to his father, he posted the property and refused to allow any logging on his land.

"So what are you planning to do with this little guy?" Roger asked.

"I don't know. I just couldn't leave him there. Could you keep him at your place?"

"I suppose I could, but I don't have time to care for him. Maybe if you came by, once in a while to help, we could give it a try," Roger replied.

She saw right through Roger's ploy, but that was fine with her. In high school, Roger had been very forgettable; now she knew she would think of no one else.

They took the fawn to Roger's cabin by canoe. Over the next few weeks, they were together regularly, caring for the fawn and taking long walks in the woods. They grew closer and more inseparable with each passing day. When the fawn was old enough to survive on its own, they led it deep into the state-owned forest and set it free. Then they walked back toward the cabin, hand-in-hand, without speaking. When they reached the banks of the Jessup River, not far from where they had found the fawn, Roger dropped down to one knee and proposed marriage.

For the next thirty-five years, they lived a simple, but happy life in the mountains. Roger was always quick to say they did not live off the land, they lived in harmony and rhythm with the land. A little renewable forestry, some simple crops, a few chickens and goats, and they managed to get by. They raised two children, Richard and Carolyn, and somehow they managed to survive when Richie was killed in a car accident when he was only eighteen.

Roger had always been larger-than-life to her, but the leukemia took him quickly. The doctors suggested new experimental treatments, but Roger refused. When he left the hospital for the last time, he told the doctors he was not going home to die, he was going home to live in the only place where he ever felt truly alive. She cared for him as she always had, with love and respect, trusting that he was doing the right thing. She hated watching him die, but after living life with him, she knew that this was the only way. Roger died in his sleep, with Abigail at his side and the peace of the Adirondacks all around him. It took a special permit from the state, but she buried him on a knoll overlooking their special place on the Jessup River.

Now, seven years after Roger died, another man in a canoe has paddled into her life at a time when she wondered how she was going to get through one more winter alone. It may be coincidence; it may be too little, too late or it may be an answer to her incessant prayers. Whatever it was, for the first time in months, she could smile as she turned off the lights and went to sleep.

Chapter Three

R afford and Abigail settled into a comfortable routine over the next few days. They shared meals and friendly conversation after dinner but during the rest of the day, they worked steadily on the long list of projects to be done before the mountain winter set in. They worked independently, most of the time, but whenever Rafford needed another pair of hands Abigail proved more than competent. Together, they patched the barn roof, scraped and painted the shingles on the north side of the house, overhauled the well pump and managed to get the old Kubota tractor running well enough to power the snowplow. Rafford was amazed by the woman's stamina. She always had breakfast ready before he got up, she worked hard all day but was never too tired to be sociable at dinner. He wondered how old she was, but knew better than to ask. Watching her, he could not help but admire her and hope to be equally self-sufficient when he was her age.

The dog, Smokey, never left Abigail's side. He allowed Rafford to share her attention, and even pretended to enjoy Rafford scratching him behind the ears, but it was clear that he was Abigail's dog. Rafford noticed she talked to Smokey constantly, not treating him like a dog but instead speaking in a sweet and gentle voice as if confiding in an old friend.

After dinner on the fourth night, they were having coffee in the kitchen and the conversation lagged. Rafford reached for the work list Abigail kept on the wall near the telephone.

Abigail spoke first, "We've made real progress in the past few days."

"Yes, we have," Rafford answered, "but there is still so much to do, and that patch we put on the roof over the hayloft is not going to hold. The wind last night ripped the tarp pretty bad; it really needs a more permanent fix. A couple of sheets of ply score and some new shake shingles would be the best."

"Can you do that kind of work – I mean alone?" she added with a smile.

"I think I can do it, but I would need help. Probably a couple of days work, if the weather cooperates," Rafford replied.

Abigail seemed to hesitate, for a moment, then said, "OK, take the truck into town tomorrow and get the materials. Larry at the Agway may be able to find a man to work with you. Also, I need you to pick up some barbed wire and a dozen fence posts."

"What is the fencing for? I don't see it on the list."

"I need you to mend the fence line on the north side," Abigail said.

"OK, but I didn't think your property was fenced."

"It's not – only on the north side."

"Abigail, is there something I don't know about? Why do you have barbed wire on the north side?" Rafford was curious now.

"It's just the rod and gun club. Those yahoos are a thorn in my side. When they are done shooting at everything that moves on their land, they like to wander onto mine. A few weeks ago, one of them took a shot at old Smokey, – claimed he thought the dog was a bear! They never paid any attention to the posted signs, so I put up a fence. Lately, the fence hasn't stopped them either; somehow, the fencing mysteriously gets cut or pulled down. Anyway, I'd like you to walk the fence line and fix what needs fixing."

Rafford stared at the list and said, "Abigail, I'm starting to wonder how much of this I can get done before I go. Unless you want company for the winter, we probably should set some priorities."

The silence lingered between them for a moment before she answered, "I suppose you're right. This old place has been crumbling for a long time. We can't fix everything in a few days. How much longer can you stay – I don't want to keep you from your job in Normantown."

"Well, my job, if it comes through, depends on the weather. I'm going to see a guy about working at a cross-country ski center – grooming trails, maintenance work, that kind of stuff. It's not real definite, just a referral from a guy I met up in Tupper Lake."

"Rafford, I don't know how much he was going to pay you, but would you consider staying on here? There is plenty of work to do and I can offer you..."

"Abigail," he interrupted, "I have really enjoyed being here for the past few days, and I would be happy to stay for the winter, if you really want me to; but I can't take your money. Room and board is good pay for the work I do. I can probably pick up some odd jobs, around, to put a little cash in my pocket."

"Nonsense! Indentured servitude was outlawed a long time ago. I can afford to pay you, at least as well as some ski center in Normantown – no one in their right mind would go there in the winter, anyway. So if you are willing to stay, you've got a job for the winter!"

"Well, OK, I guess you've got yourself a hired hand! I really do like it here; thank you for keeping me on."

After breakfast the next morning, Abigail handed him the keys to the pickup truck and two hundred dollars in cash for the roofing and fencing materials.

"At the end of the driveway, turn left. Seven or eight miles down the road, you'll come to Route 30. Cold River is about 4 miles north of the intersection. Don't blink your eyes or you will miss the entire town. If you're not back by lunch time, I'll send Smokey out looking for you!" she said with a smile.

The morning was crisp and clear and the air smelled of pine tinged with wood smoke. Rafford eased the pickup down the rutted driveway as he tried to get a feel for the clutch and the gearshift. Once on the road the old truck ran smoothly and Rafford remembered how much he enjoyed driving.

Not far down the road from Deer Run, he spotted the entrance to the Black Stag Rod and Gun Club. The dirt road to the club was marked with only a small sign, but a garish display of deer antlers made it hard to miss. Dozens of sets of antlers were nailed to two tall poles, one on either side of the dirt road. Rafford had seen too many of these clubs in the Adirondacks – secretive hideaways for wannabe woodsmen, all too often fueled by a dangerous combination of alcohol and testosterone. Why some men constantly tried to prove their manhood with guns and booze was beyond him. He made a mental note to ask Abigail more about her gun club neighbors.

Just past the "Welcome to Cold River" sign, he stopped at Lou's Country Corner for gas and a cup of coffee. It was a typical country store, with a little bit of everything – gas, groceries, bait, even T-shirts and caps for the tourists. He sat at the lunch counter and Lou, herself, poured his coffee. When he paid his bill, he picked out a couple of blueberry muffins for Abigail.

As soon as he had the truck back on the road, Rafford noticed flashing red lights in his rearview mirror. He pulled over onto the shoulder of the road and stopped.

A slightly overweight middle-aged man in a khaki Sheriff's uniform approached the driver's side of the truck and said, "License and registration, please."

Rafford removed his driver's license from his wallet and handed it through the open window. "I'm not sure about the registration," he said as he fumbled around in the glove compartment.

"Step out of the truck, please, and keep your hands where I can see them," the Sheriff had an edge in his voice.

"Is there a problem, officer?" Rafford asked. "I'm sure the registration is here, if you'll just give me a minute –"

"Just get out of the truck, now!"

Rafford eased out of the truck and noticed that the Sheriff's hand rested on the butt of his gun. Rafford moved very slowly and made sure he kept his hands in plain view. As he closed the door, a battered gray pickup truck pulled in behind the Sheriff's car and an old man with a white beard got out and hurried toward them.

"That's him, Curtis!" the old man called out, "and that's her truck!"

"All right, Amos; I know that's her truck," the Sheriff answered without looking away from Rafford.

"Rafford Brown", the Sheriff read from the driver's license, "is that right?"

Rafford nodded, "Yes sir."

"Well, Mr. Brown" the Sheriff continued, "you've got some explaining to do. Your driver's license has expired, you're a long way from home, and you're driving a truck that don't belong to you."

The old man interrupted, "The money – don't forget about the wad of bills, Curtis!"

"Shut up, Amos! I know what I'm doing," the Sheriff barked at the old man. "Are you carrying any weapons, Mr. Brown?"

"No, sir" Rafford answered.

"What about drugs or needles?" the Sheriff continued.

"No drugs or needles either. Look, I can explain –"

"All in due time. First, I want you to put your hands on the fender, and spread your feet – now!" the Sheriff's voice was firm and insistent, but Rafford could tell he did not do this often.

The Sheriff patted him down, armpits, pockets and pant legs, especially near his boots, then removed the money from his front pocket and counted it out. "Two hundred and twenty four dollars; that's a lot of money to be carrying around."

"The money is –" Rafford started to explain.

The Sheriff interrupted, "Hold on! Let's do this by the book. Is this your truck?"

"No, it isn't mine," Rafford answered. "It belongs to Abigail Sherwood. She gave it to me –"

This time the old man interrupted, "Ha! Gave it to you – never, not a chance!"

The Sheriff jerked his head around toward the old man, "Amos, if you don't keep your mouth shut, I'm gonna arrest you!"

Rafford tried again, "Sheriff, I was trying to say that Mrs. Sherwood gave me the truck to run some errands. I'm doing some work for her and needed supplies from the Agway. That's what the money is for – shingles, fencing and such."

"Why didn't you use your own vehicle?"

Rafford hesitated; somehow, he did not think the Sheriff would understand if he told him he had arrived at Deer Run in a canoe. "I needed a truck to carry the supplies," he answered.

"We'll see about that. Right now, put your hands behind your back; I'm going to put the cuffs on you."

"Am I under arrest, Sheriff?"

"It's just until we sort this out," he answered as the handcuffs clicked shut around Rafford's wrists.

Sitting in the backseat of the Sheriff's car, Rafford could hear the Sheriff on the radio. "Olivia, see if you can patch me through to Abigail Sherwood out at Deer Run. I'll wait; it's important."

"Abigail – its Curtis Coleman. Are you all right?" Rafford could faintly hear Abigail's voice through the radio's static. "No

– I mean, I'm glad to hear that. Anyway, I've got your pick-up here – there's a stranger driving it claiming that you gave him money and the truck to get supplies at –"

The Sheriff never finished his sentence; he was cut-off by a shout followed by a shrill tirade. Abigail was giving the Sheriff a real tongue-lashing.

"Well, I've got him cuffed, but he's not under arrest –"

Again, the Sheriff could not finish his sentence. He held the radio away from his ear and winced. Then he gave the other man, Amos, a stern look.

"OK, Abigail, I understand. I was just doing my job, looking out for you –"

Rafford heard another outburst from the radio.

"OK. Goodbye." There was a loud click before the Sheriff finished his words.

"Sheriff," Amos began.

"Not one word, Amos! I swear to God above," Sheriff Coleman stammered for words "Just keep quiet, for once in your life."

The Sheriff took off the handcuffs and returned the money to Rafford. "I could charge you for that expired license, but I've heard enough from Abigail Sherwood for one day! I'm sorry for the trouble."

Rafford got back in the truck and once again headed for the Agway store. He could not help but smile and shake his head as he thought about the way Abigail had handled the Sheriff.

At the Agway, he quickly purchased the supplies and loaded them in the back of the truck. Larry, at the counter, said he knew someone who could use the work and promised to send him by the next day to help with the roofing. Larry was smiling the whole time as they talked, as if he knew some secret. As Rafford was paying the bill, he heard the squawk of a two-way radio, followed by the now familiar voice of Sheriff Coleman talking to the dispatcher. Suddenly, Rafford understood the smirk on Larry's face. He had a scanner, and that meant that he, and who knew how many others, had heard Abigail rip into the Sheriff!

"Curtis is having a tough day," he said to Rafford with a grin, as he handed him his receipt.

Chapter Four

Rafford thought that Abigail seemed distant and distracted all through dinner; they hardly spoke at all, except for sharing a good laugh about the Sheriff. Rafford tried to tell her about the repair plans for the barn, but nothing he said appeared to interest her.

"Abigail, is something wrong? You don't seem yourself tonight," he said.

She slowly stirred her coffee without looking at him.

After a long silence, she said, "It's just family troubles. I had an argument with Carolyn – my daughter – today. You'd think that two grown women could get along, but we always seem to fall back into old habits. It's the dark side of the mother-daughter relationship: she tells me her troubles, I try to solve her problems and then she complains that I'm trying to run her life. It's been the same ever since she turned fourteen; after all these years we have every move down to a choreographed routine!"

"What happened when she was fourteen?" Rafford asked with some trepidation.

"She got her first boyfriend, of course! From that moment on, she's wanted to be her own person – and she has been, for the most part. But every time something in her life goes bump, she comes back to me and we start this awkward dance that mothers and daughters learn from each other.   I suppose it must be the same with fathers and sons..."

Rafford thought about his father, "Yeah, I guess it is – although it's probably not so much a dance – it's more like a barroom brawl for us. You know, grunting, grappling and a few wild swings that seldom hit home but manage to get everybody riled-up. Of course, every once in a while someone lands a sucker punch and then watch out!"

Abigail nodded her head and gave him a half-smile, "Well, I think I hit home today, with Carolyn, and I feel terrible about it. She called to tell me that she and Tyler, her boy, were coming for Thanksgiving. That part was fine, actually, since I usually go to her place in Boston for the holidays and I would much rather have them here. Then she said she wanted to leave Tyler here with me until Christmas, so she could go down to Texas to look for a new job. Well, I couldn't let that go by, not without reminding her about her responsibilities as a mother. It didn't take long for me to hit my stride and, by the time I was done, I made it sound like she was abandoning the boy on a street corner. This time I think I went too far."

"How old is Tyler?"

"He's ten – and he's a good boy, in spite of..." Abigail stopped in mid-sentence, and then started again, "You know, he is a good boy, so she must be doing something right. She's raised him on her own and that's not an easy thing to do, these days. God forgive me! I'm so quick to point out her faults."

Rafford didn't know what else to say. He was not about to give anyone advice when it came to children and families. He decided the best thing he could do was to listen.

However, Abigail was done talking, at least for now. She took a deep breath and seemed to gather herself, and then she rose and started clearing the dinner table. A comfortable silence settled over them as Rafford washed the dishes and Abigail organized the kitchen.

Finally, Abigail said to no one in particular, "It will be good to have Tyler here for a while."

In the morning, Rafford headed straight for the barn after breakfast. He had planned the roof repair down to the last detail, double-checking the supplies and his tools. Yesterday, he had prepared the roof, cleared away the rotted wood and reinforced one of the rafters that had started to decay from constant exposure to wind and water. He was ready.

As he gathered his tools, Rafford heard a car rolling up the gravel driveway. He was surprised to see the gray pickup truck that belonged to the old man who had called the Sheriff on him. *What in the world does he want? Is he checking up on me? Maybe he is here to see Abigail, because he seemed like he was sweet on her.* He watched him get out of the truck and noticed he was carrying a toolbox. Suddenly the truth hit Rafford like a low blow – this was his helper for the roof!

"Mornin'?" the old man called. "I hear you got work to do? Larry, at the Agway sent me? Name's Amos Kreal?" Although, the old man's voice inflection went up in pitch at the end of everything he said, as if he was asking a question, he got no response from Rafford.

"Look, about yesterday, I'm real sorry I called the Sheriff. It's just, well Abigail Sherwood is... well, I wouldn't want anything bad to..." he seemed to be struggling to find the right words. Finally, he blurted out "Look if you're still sore, I understand. I'll just head on home and you can ask Larry to find someone else."

"No," Rafford said, "I just wasn't expecting you. No hard feelings."

Rafford walked over to him and shook his hand. "C'mon around back, and I'll show you what needs to be done. The toughest part will be handling the ply score sheets and the bundles of shakes – they're pretty heavy..."

"I may be old, Mr. Brown, but I still know how to work," Amos said matter-of-factly.

"OK, Amos – and call me Rafford, Mr. Brown was my father."

The two men worked steadily all morning, hauling materials up into the loft and gradually fitting them in place. Amos worked hard, for a man of any age. He had worked with shake shingles many times before and soon he was giving Rafford directions.

Around midday, they stopped for a lunch of biscuits and sausages leftover from breakfast. They ate perched on top of the barn while admiring the view. The hardwoods had shed most of their leaves by now, and through the bare branches, they could see the Jessup River winding toward the horizon.

"God, this is beautiful country," Rafford said. "Have you lived here all your life, Amos?"

"Pretty near," the old man answered. "I came to the mountains with the CCC – the Civilian Conservation Corps? That was 1938, and I been here ever since. Only time I left was during the war. I helped Roger Sherwood clear this land. He and I built this barn, together."

"No wonder you care about Abigail," Rafford replied.

"Yep, I wouldn't let no harm come to her."

In the distance, the sound of gunfire echoed across the mountains. They listened as the sound repeated several more times then fell silent.

Amos shook his head, "Has she told you about her run-ins with the gun club?"

"She told me about them cutting the fence and taking a shot at Smokey."

"That's all? She just won't take those guys seriously," Amos sounded worried. "I prob'ly shouldn't say any more – let her tell you herself – but she's so darned stubborn!"

"What else, Amos?"

"A couple of years ago, some new guys took control of the club; city fellas. They act like they think the whole Adirondack Park was put here for them. They tear through the woods on

ATVs and snowmobiles, making a god-awful racket and terrorizing the wildlife. Not just on their own land, but all through the State land and Abigail's land too. They won't admit it's them, but everybody knows. Curtis – the Sheriff – and the forest rangers have been trying to catch them, but so far, they've got away with it. Last winter they nearly killed a man who was snowshoeing up on Whitlock Ridge – they ran him right off the trail. He fell some fifty feet – broke his ankle and dislocated a shoulder. When the rangers tried to get a statement from him so they could press charges, he changed his story and said it was an accident. I don't know if they paid him off or threatened him, or what, but he refused to cooperate."

"Sounds like a bad group," Rafford agreed.

"Abigail's about the only one who stands up to them – she won't 'bide any of their excuses. She's convinced that they scout out deer, fox, bear, and other wildlife, and then use the ATVs to herd them onto gun club land. Once on their own property, they do whatever they want. That's why, after forty years without fences, Abigail put up the barbed wire on the North side. She worries more about the deer than she does about standing up to those – "

"Amos!" Abigail's shout from the barnyard below interrupted his story, "What fool nonsense are you chattering on about? I thought I was paying you to work, not sit on the roof and talk Rafford to death!"

"It's my fault, Abigail," Rafford answered. "We stopped for lunch and started swapping stories."

"Sounds to me like Amos got the best of that swap – he's doing all the talking!"

Amos gave Rafford a sly smile and said, "I guess we better get back to work before she fires us both."

They worked on the roof all afternoon. Several more times, they heard bursts of gunfire reverberate from a distance.

Neither man said anything, but each glanced toward the house where Abigail sat on the front porch.

As they were washing up, Amos said, "I guess that's it, then. Unless you've got other work for me to do? I mean that fence work is really a two man job..."

"I expect I'll get to the fence on Friday – let's see what Abigail says."

Abigail invited Amos to stay for dinner. Throughout the meal, she and Amos reminisced about their early days in the mountains, when Roger and Abigail were first married.

"Times were hard," Abigail said. "To make ends meet, Roger and Amos worked as lumberjacks for International Paper. Roger's father wouldn't have approved, but then, Roger never bothered to ask his opinion. Logging was big business in the Adirondacks back then. Millions of board feet of timber were cut, skinned and floated down to the mills at Glens Falls. The lumberjacks would canoe into the woods in the fall, and cut timber through the winter. The icy ground made it easier to drag the logs. Then the trimmed logs were winched onto horse drawn sleds, chained into place, and dragged over frozen dirt roads to the riverbank. They stacked the logs on the banks until the spring runoff. When the weather warmed and the rivers swelled with snowmelt, they floated the logs on the roiling waters down to the mills.

The men lived and worked in difficult conditions. Bitter cold temperatures and driving winter storms wore on them, but they kept working through all but the most severe weather. The logging camps were dirty, smelly places crowded with men as rough as the land they worked. Many of the loggers were Quebecois – French Canadians. They tended to stick together, especially when a fight broke out, which happened regularly. The local men, like Roger and Amos, had to watch out for each other, too."

Amos chimed in, "Abigail was one of only a handful of women in the camps – and she was the only woman at the IP camp where we worked. She signed on as a cook, but ended up being nurse, doctor, seamstress – even a priest at times praying over the sick and more than once burying the dead. Whenever a big fight broke out, she was the only one everybody trusted, so she held the bets – and earned herself a nice commission for making sure the money was handled fairly. Roger kept telling her the camp was no place for a woman, but she was not about to spend the winter without him."

Abigail picked up the story, "When I got pregnant with Richie, our days in the logging camps came to an end. Roger didn't want me to go "in my condition" and I wasn't about to let him go without me. So, we scrimped and saved and somehow we made it through. Three years later, Carolyn came along and spending the winter in an Adirondack lumber camp was no longer an option. That was when Roger and Amos began logging the hardwoods here, on our own land. They even built a small sawmill and sold furniture quality lumber to local craftsmen. They made just enough money for us to get by. Of course, Roger was his own best customer for a while, as he made most of the furniture that we still use today."

"Yep," said Amos, "those were tough times. You learned a lot about yourself and you found out quick who your real friends were. Roger Sherwood was the truest friend I ever had – and just about the best man I ever knew."

When Amos had gone home, Abigail and Rafford sat by the fireplace and talked late into the night. Her stories of her early life in the mountains fascinated him, and Abigail clearly loved talking about her Roger. Love like theirs, Rafford thought, survives forever. Roger Sherwood may have died years ago, but listening to Abigail that night, Rafford felt as though he was still very much alive.

❧❧

Chapter Five

Rafford and Amos loaded the pickup with fence posts and barbed wire on Friday morning. Smokey surprised them both when he jumped in the back of the truck. The dog had continued to warm to Rafford but usually stayed close to Abigail and to the house, but apparently not today.

They drove through the woods following an abandoned fire road most of the way. Amos explained that, years ago, when the state maintained an active fire tower on Hart Mountain, the road had seen regular use. Now it was little more than a wide path through the trees but it sufficed for the old truck.

The forest along the road told a story repeated throughout the Adirondacks. A hundred years ago, conifers like pine, spruce and fir grew in scattered clumps among the dominant hardwood maples, birches, and silver beech. Then settlers and loggers arrived and clear-cut the forest lusting after the valuable hardwoods. The conifers were little more than scrap, until much later when the pulp mills down river provided a market for the soft wood. From the beginning, it was the magnificent hardwoods that made the arduous and often treacherous work worthwhile. Once they had stripped a section of forest, the loggers moved on, leaving behind only stumps and piles of bark. New growth quickly reappeared, but the faster growing evergreens swiftly filled the empty space, choking out most of the new hardwoods. A few hardwood saplings would fight their way through, but they were outmatched. By the time widespread logging ended, the Adirondack forests were predominantly evergreens, much like the forest that Rafford and Amos passed through on this November morning.

The two men rolled on in silence; for once, Rafford thought, Amos had nothing to say. When a small stream cut across the road, they parked the truck, unloaded a coil of barbed wire and some basic tools and then proceeded on foot. Smokey trailed behind them, sniffing and investigating every scent in his path. Amos knew the land well and he quickly led them to the fence line. The fence ran the length of the northern property line, from the banks of the Jessup River to highway. With the Jessup to the West, the highway to the East and the northern fence, only the southern property line remained open. The state lands to the South were part of the "forever wild" Adirondack wilderness and saw little use, only an occasional hunter or winter snowshoer.

As they walked the fence line, Rafford regularly scanned the woods on the opposite side of the fence. The gun club property looked no different than Abigail Sherwood's land – if not for the fence and the frequent "Posted" signs, the property line would have been indistinguishable. If anything, the fencing looked out of place, artificially dividing land that nature intended as one unified landscape.

"Up ahead is where the trouble has been," Amos said, gesturing toward a flat open space in the woods.

As if to prove Amos right, they found the barbed wire cut off at the posts, and patterns of tire tracks zigzagged across the soft damp earth. Rafford knelt to examine the tracks more closely.

"Don't take a tracker to know, them's ATV tracks," Amos said dryly.

"No, it doesn't," answered Rafford, "but what else do you see?"

Amos looked closer, "Well, the tracks are smooth – not many sharp edges, so I'd guess they weren't made today – could be a couple of days ago, maybe more."

"Right – and what about this area that looks like it's been wiped clean?"

The old man thought for a moment, "Looks like they were dragging something, but why? They wouldn't care about wiping out their tracks."

Rafford gently ran his fingers through the dirt and pine needles, looking for something. Then he found it – a small tuft of hair caked with mud.

Amos recognized it, "They was draggin' a deer!"

"I bet if we followed these tracks, we'd find where they gutted it – safely on gun club land." Rafford's voice was firm and tinged with anger.

Rafford let his eyes follow the ATV tracks through the gap in the fence line, and then with a start, he jumped to his feet.

"Smokey! Smokey, come here boy!" he called, but the dog did not respond. He had his nose to the ground and he was moving at a determined trot, straight into the woods on the gun club side of the fence. Rafford hesitated only a second.

"Amos, wait here!" he shouted over his shoulder as he ran through the gap in the fencing where Smokey had disappeared in the underbrush.

Rafford followed the dog moving quickly, but quietly, hunched over as he ran. Without warning, a gunshot rang out and Rafford instinctively dropped to one knee. The sound of the shot echoed off the rocks and the hillside, making it impossible to know where the shot came from. Rafford started moving forward again, crouched low to the ground, his eyes searching the woods on all sides for some sign of Smokey or the shooter. He had taken only a few steps when a second shot rang out; this one clipped a tree branch, just over his head. They were not shooting at Smokey they were shooting at him!

"Hey! That was too close!" he called out and then slowly stood up.

Rafford heard the ATV before he saw it. As it came closer, he saw the lone rider, and the rifle. The man wore a full set of camouflage – shirt, pants and boonie hat – all that was missing was the green and black commando make-up. Rafford guessed that this guy probably had that, too.

"Sorry, friend," the rider said after the four-wheeler rolled to a stop. "I had a bead on a good size turkey, when he spooked and took to the air. I didn't expect anyone to be here - this is private land, you know."

"Yeah, private land – only my dog can't read, and he came through a gap someone cut in the fence, over there. I'm just trying to get him back."

Right at that moment, as if on cue, Smokey came lumbering through the underbrush.

"Well, you both should be more careful. We wouldn't want anybody getting shot. So you came over from the widow's place – you a friend of hers?" the man asked.

Rafford eyed him suspiciously. "I'm doing some work for her. You know, cutting wood, fixing the roof, mending fence."

"I wouldn't waste my time with that fence, if I were you. Barbed wire just don't belong in the woods. Besides, it just ain't neighborly."

Rafford wanted to knock the smirk off the man's face, but this was not the time. "Well you know what Robert Frost said about fences and neighbors..."

"No, I don't believe I do," the man said.

"Oh," Rafford replied without expression on his face. "Come on, Smokey, we got fences to mend, and miles to go before we sleep."

"Hey, you remember what I said about trespassing..."

Rafford turned very deliberately and gave him a stony look, then, without speaking, walked back to the fence-line with Smokey. At first, Amos was nowhere to be seen, then Rafford spotted him running towards him carrying a shotgun.

"Sweet Jesus – are you alright?" Amos, wheezed as he tried to speak and catch his breath, at the same time. "I heard gun shots, so I ran to get the shotgun from the truck. What happened?"

"I just had a friendly chat with one of the neighbors. Any more like him and this neighborhood will just go to ruin."

The two men sat down on a large boulder and Rafford told Amos the whole story.

"Any idea who this guy might be?"

"Probably, George Harder – he's the caretaker for the gun club. Not too bright and he's pretty full of himself since the new owners started throwing their weight – and their money – around. He used to run the town landfill, before it was sealed. He's more stupid than dangerous; anyway, he's not the problem over there, he just works for them."

The two men spent the rest of the day repairing the fence. In just over a mile of fencing, they found three places where the barbed wire had been cut away. ATV tracks were plainly visible in each spot, not only near the fence but throughout the woods. In one area, they followed the ATV tracks deep into Abigail's land.

Early in the afternoon, the temperature dropped suddenly, and both men intuitively looked to the western sky. Gray clouds rolling steadily eastward could mean only one thing, this time of year.

"Snow tonight," Amos said matter-of-factly.

Rafford nodded in agreement, "Let's head back. I want to start-up that old tractor, before the sun goes down. We may need the snowplow in the morning."

"I know a shortcut," Amos said as he left the fence-line and headed directly into the woods.

They bushwhacked in silence for about 20 minutes, scrambling over downed trees and ducking under low-hanging limbs. Suddenly, Amos stopped, grabbed Smokey's collar with one hand and raised his other hand signaling Rafford to be quiet. Ahead of them, a doe was drinking from a small stream. Every few seconds, she raised her head looking first to one side then the other. The men watched in silence for two or three minutes, then the doe slowly wandered off. Her rounded belly rolled side to side and gave her a comical swaying gait as she walked away.

Amos circled away from the deer, and when they had safely crossed the stream, he turned to Rafford and spoke, "Well, I'll be, I've never seen a pregnant doe this time of year!"

"No – me either. That fawn's going to have a rough time getting through the winter."

"Whatever you do, don't tell Abigail! She'll have us out here playing midwife," Amos said with a grin.

The snow started after supper that evening, and by the time Rafford turned in for the night he knew the Kubota would get a good workout in the morning. The big fluffy flakes drifted gracefully through the quiet night. Rafford put an extra log in the woodstove and quickly fell asleep.

He woke shortly after daybreak, and looked out the window to see the ground covered by at least a foot of virgin powdery snow. A few flakes hung in the air, but the storm seemed to be over. As he dressed, he heard Smokey barking. Abigail must be up early today, he thought. When he opened the tack room door, he spotted Smokey half-buried in snow near the house. The dog was digging around in the drifts, and every so often would bury his face in the snow and come up snorting the snowflakes from his snout.

"Smokey!" he called, "you old fool. You're not a puppy anymore; you've seen snow before!"

The dog looked in his direction, barked twice and went back to pawing at the snow, then looked up and barked again.

"What have you got, there?" Rafford said as he walked toward the excited dog.

As he neared the house, the form in the snow ominously took shape. Abigail lay at the bottom of the porch steps, partially covered with snow, wearing only a flannel nightgown and slippers.

"Abigail!" Rafford shook her gently, but she did not respond.

He quickly checked for signs of injury, but found nothing. He knew it was risky to move her, but her skin was cold and her pulse weak. Supporting her head with his arm, he gently picked her up and carried her into the house. He was surprised at how easily he could lift her – she seemed to weigh nothing at all. He laid her on the sofa in the living room and covered her with the woolen blanket from her favorite rocking chair.

The Cold River Volunteer Ambulance Squad responded quickly and Sheriff Coleman pulled in right behind them. While the EMTs worked on Abigail, Sheriff Coleman took Rafford aside.

"So you found her outside?" the sheriff asked, suspiciously.

"Yes – actually Smokey found her at the bottom of the porch steps. I don't know how long she was there. I didn't see any sign of injury, so I carried her in here to get warm."

Rafford watched the volunteers care for Abigail, checking vital signs and gently massaging her arms and legs. Rafford realized Coleman was speaking again.

"...and you didn't hear anything?"

"Huh – no, I mean I heard Smokey barking when I was getting dressed, but other than that – no I didn't hear a thing. "

On the sofa, Abigail moaned softly, and tried to open her eyes. Coleman went to the couch and knelt near her head, listening, but she was lapsing in and out of consciousness. One of the ambulance volunteers was talking on a two-way radio while another started an IV line in Abigail's left arm. The one starting the IV said something to Sheriff Coleman, and then Coleman got up and approached Rafford.

"They say she is doing OK, but they are going to take her to the hospital in Tupper Lake. She has a nasty bump on the back of her head and her body temperature is low – our guess is that she slipped on the steps and hit her head on the way down."

Rafford nodded, "That makes sense. I'll pack a few things for her and follow the ambulance up to Tupper."

By the time Rafford was allowed to see Abigail in the hospital, she was fully awake and giving everybody a piece of her mind, especially the young doctor who refused to let her go home. She was sitting up in the hospital bed trying to remove the IV line when Rafford walked in.

"Abigail, what do you think you are doing?" his voice startled her. "Stop picking at that tape – you need that IV, at least for now."

She glared at him for a moment then her mood softened from anger to resignation. Rafford knew she would listen to him.

"I packed a few things that I thought you might want."

"I don't plan to be here that long. In fact, I should be home right now!" she barked.

"Calm down – you've had a tough morning. Let the doctors check you over and as soon as you are released, I will be here to take you home."

"Doctors? This doctor looks like he just got out of high school! He's still got pimples, for goodness sake! What does he know about how I feel?"

"Look, I'm sure he knows what he is doing. Just give him a chance, and I'll bet you'll be home in no time."

The doctor came back into the room and looked a little relieved to see Rafford smile at him. His smile was involuntary; Abigail was right – the doctor did look like a teenager, right down to his pimples. Rafford suppressed the urge to laugh, and gave Abigail a look that silently said please cooperate. Abigail just rolled her eyes at him.

"Mrs. Sherwood, I know you don't want to be here, but I want you to stay overnight for observation." Without giving Abigail a chance to tell him what she thought of that idea, he continued, "Your body temperature is back in the normal range, but I am still concerned about the lump on the back of your head."

He took her hand and touched her fingers to the swelling near the base of her skull. "Can you feel that? I want to see if the swelling goes down overnight. I expect it will and then you can go home in the morning. If it doesn't go down, then I would worry about a more serious injury, and we would want to do some more testing. You are a very lucky woman, Mrs. Sherwood – between hitting your head and having a very close call with hypothermia, you could easily have suffered permanent injuries, even death. Compared with those options, I'm sure you'll agree, a night in the hospital is just a small inconvenience."

After the doctor left, Abigail said with a half-smile, "Well, maybe he was one of those boy geniuses."

Rafford wanted to ask her what she remembered about her fall, but Sheriff Coleman walked in. Rafford guessed he probably intended to ask the same question.

"Abigail, you're looking better than when I saw you a few hours ago," the Sheriff said as he turned toward Rafford. "Would you give me a couple of minutes with Abigail, alone, please?"

The Sheriff walked Rafford to the door and closed it after him.   "Abigail, do you remember what happened this morning?"

"Of course, I do!" Abigail did not like being patronized. "I got up about sun-up, as usual, and let Smokey out. I saw a hawk circling over the barn and figured he was after my chickens. So I went to the top of the steps and waved my arms at him. The next thing I know, I was strapped down on a stretcher in the back of Ralph's ambulance. I guess I must have slipped on the steps and fallen."

"Well, it looked like an accident to us, too, but I just wanted to be sure that Rafford's story checked out."

"Rafford – is that what this is about? You think that he – Curtis, that badge doesn't give you the right to go around accusing good people."

"Now, Abigail, I'm not accusing anybody of anything, but this guy – well, he just appears out of nowhere. I mean what do you know about him?"   Before she could answer he continued, "Nothing! And I've done some checking-up on him, and I tell you something's not right."

"You've been checking up on Rafford?"

"It's my job, Abigail, I am the gosh-darned Sheriff! After we stopped him driving your truck, I ran his license through the state police computer, but he's something of a mystery. Until about two years ago, he was living in Saratoga Springs working for some environmental company. Then, suddenly, he just drops out of sight – his house is sold, his licenses, even his state professional registrations, expire and they are not renewed. He vanishes for more than two years and then he shows up on your doorstep. Something's not right, Abigail, and by God, I'm gonna find out about your Rafford Brown."

"Curtis, I understand you are the Sheriff, and you're right, I don't know much about Rafford; but what little I do know is important. I know he' got a good heart, he works hard and he has been a great help to me over the past couple of weeks.

Most importantly, I know that if he had not been there this morning, this conversation would be pretty one-sided, because I would have died in that snowdrift. Curtis, he saved my life this morning, and that has got to count for something."

The Sheriff nodded in agreement, "Yes, he did save your life, and I must admit from what I've seen, he is a decent man. But I have to find out what happened before he came here, and I will. Until then, please be careful and if he tells you anything that would explain all of this, call me."

"Thank you for your concern. Would you send Rafford back in, on your way out? I've got some chores for him to do while I am cooped up in here."

Abigail was clearly done talking.

‿‿

Chapter Six

R afford felt like an intruder as he walked through Abigail's darkened home. He had spent many hours with her in the kitchen and occasionally in front of the living room fireplace, but he had never strayed into the rest of the house. Now, on her orders, he moved from room to room, checking to be sure that everything was all right.

The first floor held few secrets. However, he noticed, for the first time, how the furniture, photographs and memorabilia combined to present a vivid picture of Abigail and Roger together. It gave the impression that they had always been together and always here, in this house.

The house, and the furniture that Roger had built for it, had a solid, enduring quality that Rafford found very reassuring. He wished that he had known Roger. Whenever Abigail spoke of their life together, he could hear her love for him in every word. She called him her rock; the foundation of her life. Even when she spoke of his final illness, it was without any trace of anger or regret, as if his death was simply one more part of the treasured life they had shared. Roger had lived a full and rich life to the very end; a life inextricably intertwined with Abigail and with this particular place in the Adirondacks.

Rafford moved up the stairs to the second floor. He knew that Abigail usually slept in a small room on the first floor, just off the living room, but he immediately recognized the bedroom at the top of the stairs that she had shared with Roger. The beautiful four-poster bed that dominated the room had to be Roger's handiwork; like the furniture on the first floor, it embodied simple elegance. Rafford ran his fingertips along the flowing lines of the headboard and up the strong but graceful posts and finials; the richness of the hand-finished oak begged to be touched.

He looked around the room and found repeated evidence of Roger's craftsmanship accented by Abigail's finishing touches: the oak window seat with its delicately embroidered cushion, the bentwood rocker draped with a crocheted afghan, the dark pine blanket chest with a doe and fawn hand-painted on the lid. The presence of Roger and Abigail was palpable, to the point that Rafford felt he was trespassing. He backed out of the room, quietly and respectfully, and then moved down the hall.

The other upstairs rooms held no surprise. Two bedrooms that probably once belonged to the children now waited expectantly for guests. A third bedroom served as Abigail's sewing room, although it appeared little used.

Walking back to the stairs, his eyes drifted to the family photo gallery that lined the hallway. Simply framed photographs of Richard and Carolyn clustered carefully to reveal the awkward progression of each from infant to teenager. Rafford remembered that Richard had died at 18. Was it merely coincidence that there were no pictures of Carolyn after her teen years? Even though he knew it was none of his business, he wanted to understand Abigail and her family. He felt drawn to all of them; as if he were some distant relative, returned after a long absence.

Downstairs, where he felt more at ease, he found a pillow and a handmade down comforter in the hall closet. He would keep his promise and spend the night in the house – but not in the guest room as Abigail had instructed. He would sleep on the living room couch.

Rafford lay sleepless for what seemed a long while. Several times he dozed off, but slept fitfully, tossing and turning and waking again with every creak and groan of the old house. Exhausted, he finally fell into a deep sleep just before dawn. That was when the dream came, just as it had come dozens of times before. As soon as he saw her face, he knew what would happen just as he knew that he was powerless to stop it.

In his dream, she was walking a few steps ahead of him without a care in the world. Her blond pigtails bounced with each step, brushing lightly against the base of her neck. She looked just as she did in the picture that he carried in his Bible and, watching her, he could not help but smile. She was everything to him: the sun, the moon and the stars. Before she was born he had no idea that he could love anyone this way – totally, unconditionally, with every breath he took. Four years as Casey's father had completely changed his life.

He followed her along the narrow dream-world path quickening his steps, trying to catch-up with her. How could those tiny legs keep her so far ahead? He began to run, but he still could not close the gap. She remained well beyond his reach.

Ahead he saw the low stone wall that marked the edge of the ravine. He strained to run faster, but his legs were too heavy; they seemed to move in slow motion as though churning through deep sand. Helplessly, he watched Casey approach the wall. He tried to call her name; his lips moved but no sound came from his mouth. Suddenly, she was standing on top of the wall. She turned to face him and her sweet innocent smile was the last thing he saw as she fell backwards and disappeared into the darkness beyond.

He raced to the wall and looked over, searching frantically for her; but he could see no trace. The ravine, seemed to fall away into dark nothingness. Casey had disappeared, swallowed up by the blackness. He heard his own voice scream her name, but there was no answer. Frantic, he climbed to the top of the wall, took one last look and jumped.

He awoke, gasping for air, and looked anxiously around the darkened room confused and disoriented. The dream always ended the same way; he never reached the bottom of the chasm and he never saw his daughter again. She always remained just beyond his reach and she always vanished into the darkness where he could not follow.

The sound of the telephone ringing shattered the silence and startled him. He hesitated, not sure if he should answer. What would he say about Abigail, and how would he explain him being in her house? He looked at the clock – 6:45am – and he immediately knew who was calling. He picked up the receiver, and before he could speak, he heard her voice.

"What took you so long? I was about ready to send Curtis to check on you!"

"Good morning, Abigail. You sound like you're feeling better," Rafford said, forcing a smile.

"Of course, I'm better - but if you don't come and get me out of here soon I'll be headed to the funny farm!"

"Abigail, you haven't even been there 24 hours - when the doctor..."

She interrupted him, "He said I can go home. Come and get me, if you leave right now, we can be home in time for lunch. The food in this place is disgusting!"

"It's 6:45 in the morning - you expect me to believe that the doctor has already made his morning rounds?"

"Mr. Brown, I don't expect you to believe anything - I just expect you to drive my truck up here and pick me up!"

Rafford knew from her tone of voice that he had crossed a line that he should not have crossed. "I'm sorry, Abigail, I just want to know that you are all right. I'll leave right away."

"Thank you. Don't forget, I was 'all right' for 68 years before you started worrying about me."

"Yes, ma'am; I'll be there right away."

Abigail was dressed, packed and sitting on the edge of the bed when Rafford arrived. Before either of them could say more than hello, a middle-aged woman carrying a Bible came into the room.

"Abigail," she said. "I am so relieved to see you sitting up and looking so well!"

"Good morning, Pastor Joanne. I didn't expect to see you here on a Sunday morning," Abigail replied.

"It's all part of the service, don't you know. If you can't come to me on a Sunday, I will track you down and come to you! How are you feeling?"

"I'm fine – it will take more than a bump on the head to stop me. Rafford was just going to drive me home. Oh, I'm sorry, this is Rafford Brown – he's working for me now, but I haven't been able to get him to church, yet."

"Mr. Brown, I'm Joanne Farber, Abigail's pastor. Welcome to our community and thank you! I hear I have you to thank for pulling Abigail back from the brink. I don't know what we would do without her."

Rafford nodded and smiled but said nothing.

Abigail broke the silence, "I'm sorry you had to make the trip all the way up here before church. Who called you?"

"A better question would be who didn't call. It's a small town, Abigail. The word spread quickly once the ambulance was called. I would have been here yesterday but I had a wedding over in Bolton Landing and didn't get back until late last night. When I returned I must have had nearly a dozen messages on the answering machine. Everyone has been praying for you."

"I must admit, I did some praying myself," Abigail answered.

"I can imagine, especially knowing your aversion to hospitals."

"Anyway, you can tell everyone I'm on the mend and headed home. God is good!"

"All the time! It was good to meet you Rafford. I hope you will come to church with us some Sunday. Thanks for taking care of Abigail and don't hesitate to call me, if we can do anything to help."

As the pastor left, Abigail's young doctor came in with her discharge papers.

"One more day here would have made me feel better, Mrs. Sherwood, but I guess you know best. It is reassuring to know that Mr. Brown is an Emergency Medical Technician and that you will be in good hands."

Abigail caught Rafford's surprised look and gave him a look of her own that said, keep quiet. Rafford said nothing as the doctor reviewed her chart with him and told him what to watch for over the next forty-eight hours.

"If she doesn't show any symptoms over the next two days, then she should be fine." Rafford listened and nodded, knowingly.

Driving back to Deer Run, neither Rafford nor Abigail spoke until the old truck was well beyond the village line. Then Abigail broke the silence.

"After Richie's car accident, I practically lived in that hospital. He lingered in a coma for six weeks. Roger couldn't stand being there for more than a few minutes at a time, and I couldn't stand the thought of Richie being there alone. I watched him waste away, and I watched a steady parade of illness and injury pass him by, like a river of sadness and grief. I could never..." her voice trailed off.

Rafford remained silent; he did not know what to say.

Finally, she spoke again, "Anyway, I'm sorry I was short with you on the phone, and I'm sorry about the EMT business. I just had to get out of there."

"I think I understand how you feel – losing a child is so hard – the memory never goes away. But, I don't understand about the EMT business -- how did you know I used to be an EMT?"

They looked at each other and laughed long and hard. Then they drove on in silence, each lost in thoughts too private to share. When the old truck rattled across the bridge over the Jessup River, something in Abigail seemed to stir. She was almost home.

"I spoke with Carolyn last night – I didn't want her to call the house and get worried. She and Tyler will be here on Wednesday."

"How did she react to you being in the hospital?"

Abigail hesitated, "I didn't tell her where I was - no need to. I did tell her about you, just in case she wondered about the strange man sitting at our Thanksgiving table."

Now it was Rafford who hesitated, "Over Thanksgiving, I thought I might disappear for a couple of days – maybe backpack the Normantown-Placid trail along Long Lake. You know, to give you and Carolyn some time alone; holidays are family time."

"What a crock! If you want to get away from me for a couple of days, that's understandable, but don't blame it on family. However, if you're just trying to be unobtrusive, forget it. I would really like you to have Thanksgiving with my family, such as it is, but I should not have assumed that you would want to be there. So, it is up to you, but please know that you are invited."

"So what did you tell her about me? I hope you didn't use that personal EMT story again."

"No, and I'll thank you not to mention that, or anything else about the hospital, my fall or..."

"I understand. Keep Carolyn in the dark; I got it."

"So, you will join us for Thanksgiving?" she asked.

"OK, but you're not expecting me to bag a wild turkey for dinner, are you?"

Abigail's laughter was the answer he hoped for.

Smokey saw Abigail step out of the truck and ran to her barking and wagging his tail so hard that his entire body swayed side-to-side. Abigail seemed only slightly less happy to see him. In fact, Rafford was amazed how her entire demeanor changed as soon as she set foot on her own land. Her connection to this particular piece of geography was tangible.

While Abigail napped, Rafford caught up on the morning chores. Goats and chickens are creatures of habit and don't react well to changes in their routine. Once the goats were milked and all of the animals were fed and watered, he spent a couple of hours working in the barn.

When he finally went back to the house to check on Abigail, she was not on the couch, where he had left her.

"Abigail?" he called.

"Upstairs," came her reply.

He found her in one of the small bedrooms sorting through a large pile of clothes.

"While I was lying around in the hospital I remembered that I still had Roger's clothes up here, and that they would be just about your size. Don't be offended, I'm just thinking that you might need some work clothes, to save the wear and tear on your own."

"I'm not offended - if you are sure it is OK with you."

Abigail held up a lined barn coat, "Look at this! It's well broken in, but it's still got some wear left in it. Roger loved this coat." She held the coat at arm's length and gazed at it, as though she could see her husband standing before her.

"If that was a favorite, maybe I shouldn't," Rafford offered.

"Nonsense" she interrupted, "it's a barn coat, not a keepsake! Besides, it's got to be better than wearing three flannel shirts at once, like you've been doing!"

Rafford ended up with the coat, two denim shirts and a pair of bib overalls. Everything was a little tight, but serviceable. Abigail stumbled slightly when she stood up, so Rafford insisted that she rest on the couch while he made supper. She was a remarkable woman, but he was concerned that the fall might have taken something out of her. He would have to insist that she get some rest over the next couple of days - especially with company coming for Thanksgiving.

Book II – Family

In the rushing of the waters
In the whisper of the breeze
In the way the sunlight filters
Through a canopy of trees
I will always walk beside you
You'll hear me calling low
In the rumble of the thunder
In the hush of falling snow.

- For Michael
© William Delia

Chapter Seven

C arolyn eased the faded green Volvo wagon through the twists and turns of Route 30 like a true Adirondacker. Both car and driver seemed invigorated by the open roads and the crisp mountain air, grateful to be freed from the constant stops and starts that strangled Boston traffic. To generations of Adirondackers, Route 30 was the mainline that led anywhere you needed to go in the mountains; it was also the road where most of them learned to drive. Even now, as Carolyn downshifted into a sharp turn, she could hear her father's gentle reminders in her ear.

"Steady into that curve, Carolyn. Let the engine drag slow your speed, then accelerate firmly out of the turn," he would say. "Gently! Drive like there is an egg between your foot and the accelerator. Feel the tires grab the road the way your toes hold the sand on the beach. Don't be intimidated - women are naturally better drivers than men. Trust yourself."

Trust yourself.

She realized later that, somehow, nearly all of his fatherly advice came back to those same two words. Learning to drive?

Trust yourself. Boyfriend troubles? Trust yourself. Choosing a college? Trust yourself. Ending a failed marriage? Trust yourself. How many times had she gone to him hoping that he would tell her what to do, only to hear those two words? She understood what he was doing - encouraging her to be independent, to think for herself. Roger Sherwood was certainly not a man without opinions, sometimes very strong opinions, but he seemed to feel even more strongly about making her think for herself.

In the seven years since his death, she realized how well he had succeeded. As a single mother and as a woman working in the male dominated world of high-tech graphic design, his lessons gave her the confidence to keep going. Even now, as she prepared to remake her life, yet again, she knew that no matter how things turned out, she would not second-guess her decisions.

"Trust yourself and it is easy to accept the outcomes," he would say. "Doubt yourself and you will forever wonder what might have been."

This time, however, her confidence was being tested by worries about how her mother would cope with her move. Texas is much farther away than Boston and her mother is getting older. Living alone in the mountains is hard, even if you are Abigail Sherwood -- not that her mother had ever made Carolyn feel responsible for her. They spoke regularly, but seldom spoke about the difficulties that each of them faced, alone. They each made their own decisions and, if either one mentioned a problem at all, it came only in passing and usually long after it had been resolved. Carolyn and Abigail shared many traits but none more strongly than that fierce independence that Carolyn had learned from her father. She sometimes wondered if Abigail had learned it from him, too. Carolyn suspected that her mother had been born independent, but that life in the mountains with Roger Sherwood had honed her self-sufficiency to a fine edge.

Tyler stirred in the seat next to her, murmuring in some dream language. She reached across the seat and brushed the hair back off his forehead. In response, he shifted position, mumbled something, and fell silent again. He always made sounds in his sleep. As a baby, he cooed and gurgled, but now, at ten years old, he often engaged in lengthy, albeit, one-sided conversations.

Carolyn smiled as she nearly always did when she thought of him. Being Tyler's mother was one thing, maybe the only thing, that made her feel complete. Everyone told her that raising a boy, alone, would be overwhelming, but she had just charged ahead. Besides what choice did she have? Tyler's father walked out –sprinted was the way she usually described his exit – when Ty was only a few months old. So what was she to do? She would raise him, of course – alone if necessary. Potential father candidates were not exactly lining up to woo a twenty-four year-old graduate student with a baby on her hip. There were always men "sniffing around", as her friend Zoe used to say. Carolyn was not unattractive – redheads with deep green eyes were always a hot commodity on the Boston University campus – but once they caught whiff of Tyler, dubbed the 'bonus baby' by Zoe, the phone stopped ringing. After a while Carolyn became very forthright, quickly working Tyler into any conversation with a man that ventured past three or four sentences. She decided they were a package deal, so why not make that clear from the very beginning.

As an unintended result, she had discovered that she could get along just fine without a man in her life; but lately, she wasn't so sure that Tyler could. Little boys need their mothers, but every day Ty seemed less a little boy and more a mystery to Carolyn. He seemed unsure of himself, especially around other boys and their fathers. He behaved as though he felt out of place or that, perhaps, there was something wrong with him. He tried to avoid drawing attention to himself and to blend into the background. He held back, even at baseball practice, where he was easily the best player on the team. Maybe it was just a phase, and it would pass like all the others, but this one felt different to her. She hoped the move to Austin would give them each a fresh start.

She was still thinking about Tyler when elephant rock appeared on the side of the road. The happy pachyderm face painted on the large roadside boulder brought a smile to most that sped by, but not Carolyn. For her the rock served warning; "the curve" was just ahead. She eased off the accelerator, just as she always did, and her eyes automatically went to the guardrail and to the rocky riverbed beyond. A white cross, adorned with plastic flowers, stood behind a shiny new section of railing: apparently, the curve had claimed another life. She wondered how this one had died – speed, drugs, alcohol – or, was it just another logging truck on the wrong side of the road, like it had been with her brother, Richie? She still felt the ache in her stomach even after all the years. How had they survived that horrible night and the weeks of misery that followed? How had her mother found the strength to go on living after burying her son? Trying not to think the unthinkable, Carolyn rested her hand gently on Tyler's head. How?

Tyler reminded her more of Richie every day. The way he screwed up his nose and glared at her when he was angry was pure Richie. Richie had usually saved those looks for their parents, not for her. In fact, her friends were always jealous of the bond she shared with her big brother. After the accident, she had been devastated. She slept on the floor of his hospital room for days, afraid that he would die before she was able to apologize. Everyone said it was not her fault – it was an accident – but she felt responsible. He would not have been on the road that night if she had not begged him to pick her up after Sarah's party. She just had to go to Sarah Randolph's party, and Richie was not really that sick – of course, he would drive her! So she had begged and pleaded, the way only fourteen year-old girls can do and he gave in. After all, he was her big brother.

Richie's doctor had told her that some coma patients may be able to hear, even if they cannot respond. So day after day, week after week, she spent every free moment in his hospital room. She talked to him for hours, and when they were alone in the room, she would move up close to his ear and whisper how sorry she was. If he would just get better, she promised that she would never ask him to drive her anywhere, ever again. Then she would dry her eyes, and gently wipe her tears off of his pale soft cheek. Every day she cried, and every day he drifted a little farther away; every day he seemed a little less her brother. Then, he was gone.

"Mom, are you okay?" Tyler was looking at her with concern.

Carolyn wiped the tears from her cheeks with the back of her hand and smiled at him, "Well, it's about time you woke up! We're almost home."

Home, even after all the years in Boston, this was still home to her. It was more than the old house and the family memories. It was coming home to the mountains. The feelings washed over her, every time she made the drive up the long hill into Speculator. The Adirondacks would always be her home.

The Adirondacks are not as tall as the Rockies, or as dramatic as the Grand Tetons, but there is a sense of harmony here that she found nowhere else. The High Peaks, the Saranac Chain of Lakes, the Raquette River, and the Five Ponds Wilderness all seemed cut from one fabric. Even the wildlife – deer, black bear, loons, otters, eagles and the occasional moose – all shared in this sense of harmony in their mountain home.

The human residents of the Adirondacks, of course, regularly disrupted the peace of the mountains, especially within the blue line that defined the six million-acre Adirondack Park. 'Forever wild' preservationists battled with those who saw 'economic growth' as the future of the park as well as their own futures. The year-round residents found it difficult to tolerate the thousands of seasonal interlopers, especially those who treated the Adirondacks like their own personal amusement park. The seasonal residents knew, however, that tourism sustained the fragile economy of the park, so they were not at all shy about asserting their rights to be Adirondackers, too, if only for a few weeks at a time. Some of them even came to know the spirit of the mountains, and were better for the experience.

Carolyn slowed the wagon and turned carefully into Deer Run's long rutted driveway. She immediately noticed that the trees stood little taller and the house and barn drooped a little more than she remembered. This place was just too much for her mother to handle now that her father was gone. Driving up to the house and barn that her father had built with his own hands, she always thought of him. If only he were still alive, things would be different. If only...

Suddenly, there he was! He stood bent over that old Kubota tractor just as she had seen him a hundred times before with his old barn coat barely covering the rip in his overalls; the rip that she had patched with a piece of denim that she cut from a pair of her old bell-bottoms. She heard herself gasp aloud.

"Mom, look out!" Tyler yelled.

Carolyn slammed on the brakes, but it was too late. The car banged solidly into one of the fence posts on the livestock pen. They were not going fast, but the sound of shattering glass and the pronounced lean of the fence declared that damage had been done.

Before she could react, Rafford was at her car door. "Are you all right?" he asked.

Carolyn looked at his face, then at the coat and the overalls, then back to his face again. The face and the clothes did not go together, and she was bewildered.

"Who the hell are you!" she screamed as she pushed open the car door knocking Rafford back on his heels. She exploded out of the car with fire in her eyes. "What are you doing here and where did you get that coat?!"

Before he could answer, Abigail came running from the house, "Carolyn!"

She turned toward the sound of her mother's voice and her face softened, but only for a moment.

"Is this some kind of a joke?" she bellowed, her lower lip trembling and her eyes filling with tears. "If it is, it's not funny! Why is he dressed up like Daddy?"

"Carolyn, it's all right," Abigail spoke softly as she embraced her daughter. "This is Rafford Brown, the man I told you about. He works for me. What happened? Are you OK? Is Tyler OK?"

At the sound of his name, Tyler came crawling across the driver's seat and smiled at Abigail, "Hi, Grandma! Mom ran into your fence, but we're OK. Where's Smokey?"

Abigail reached out pulled him close, while still holding Carolyn with one arm. She closed her eyes and smiled as she held them, her entire family, in a firm embrace. Carolyn was still seething and Tyler would not stop squirming but Abigail was content. She did not notice when Rafford slipped away, back to the barn.

Rafford did not come to the house for dinner. Abigail had spent the afternoon with Carolyn and Tyler, helping them move into their usual rooms on the second floor, and catching up on all the happenings since she had visited them last summer. For the afternoon, Rafford was forgotten, lost in the warmth of the moment.

Abigail went onto the porch and called his name again. When he did not answer, she returned to the kitchen.

"Mom," Carolyn said, "come sit down to dinner. I'm just as glad he's not here. I mean, what do you really know about him? He just shows up here one day, and you take him in – that's dangerous! He could be –"

"For goodness sake, Carolyn!" Abigail cut her off. "I'm not senile; I know what I'm doing. Rafford Brown is a good man, and, well, without him, I don't know how I would make it through this winter. There is so much to do and without the Paige brothers I just can't keep up."

Carolyn waited a moment before replying, "Mom, just because you need him doesn't make him a good person. I worry about you, and I feel guilty that I'm not here to help. Maybe it's time to sell this place and –"

"No! This is my home and once it was yours, too. I will not move into some apartment building for old people where I can be safe and miserable. My husband and my son lived and died on this land, and I will, too. When I'm gone, do what you want, but until then, this is my home."

"It's my home, too, Mom, but right now I can't be here. I have to take care of Ty and me. As much as I would like my life to be different, sometimes things just don't work out the way we want. Sometimes we have to make choices that we don't want to make."

Abigail nodded slowly, "I know. Tyler, would you pass the mashed potatoes, please?"

They kept the rest of the dinner conversation light. Abigail asked Ty about baseball and school and teased him, repeatedly, about the fourth-grade girl who thought he was cute. After dinner, they played a quick game of Monopoly, which Tyler won after some remarkably foolish real estate deals by both his mother and his grandmother. A couple of times during the evening, Abigail glanced out the window toward the tack room, but Rafford was nowhere to be seen.

At nine o'clock, Carolyn tapped Tyler on the shoulder and said, "Time for bed, Ty. Go brush your teeth and I will come up to tuck you in."

When he had gone upstairs, Abigail spoke, "How does Tyler feel about staying with me while you go to Austin?"

"He was upset at first – not about being here but about leaving school and his friends. You know kids; he's at that age where friends are important."

"Does he have a lot of friends in Boston?"

"Sure he does," Carolyn said too quickly. "Well, maybe not a lot, but he made friends with a couple of boys from summer baseball. They go to school together and they hang out on the weekends."

"So is he unhappy about leaving them?"

"Mom, I am not going to argue with you about going to Texas. It is the right thing for us to do, right now. Tyler will make new friends, so let's not talk about this anymore."

Later, when Carolyn went upstairs to bed, Abigail went through her usual routine, turning off lights and locking doors. She looked again toward the barn and saw light coming from Rafford's window.

"I'll talk to you, tomorrow, before Thanksgiving dinner," she said softly. "I can explain about Carolyn; she's only being protective because she doesn't know you. Yes, everything will be all right, tomorrow."

Thanksgiving morning, seemed more like January than November.   Overnight, it had snowed again, covering everything with a pristine blanket of white. Abigail rose early to get the turkey ready. At nineteen pounds, the bird was much bigger than they needed, but family tradition required leftovers for turkey sandwiches and one of Abigail's famous turkey pies. She enjoyed cooking for her family and she hummed softly as she stuffed the turkey. The bird was already in the oven by the time Carolyn and Tyler came down for breakfast. Abigail had intended to speak with Rafford before breakfast, but Tyler wanted blueberry pancakes, so that came first.

Finally, at about nine-thirty, as Carolyn washed the breakfast dishes, Abigail put on her coat and headed to the barn. Smokey ran ahead of her, wagging his tail excitedly. The barn was quiet, but from the footprints in the snow, she could tell Rafford had done the morning chores. She also noticed that he had replaced the fencepost that Carolyn had driven into, yesterday. She knocked on the door to the tack room but got no answer. Abigail opened the door and could tell immediately that Rafford was not there. The wood stove was cold and his bunk was made. The clothes she had given him – the overalls, the shirts and the barn coat were in a neat pile on top of the bunk. A note pinned to the pile of clothes read, simply, "Decided to do that hike – be back on Saturday -- Rafford."

❧❧

Chapter Eight

R afford watched his Thanksgiving dinner bubble in a battered aluminum pot suspended over glowing red-gray coals. He stirred the mixture of red beans, rice and sausage, drawing the aroma deep into his lungs. Abigail is a great cook, he thought, but there is something special about a meal cooked over a campfire in the open air. The cornbread nestled in the coals needed another five minutes, so he sat back on his tree stump chair and gazed at the forest and the mountains beyond.

A wisp of smoke from his fire spiraled upward, until it vanished against the late-afternoon sky. Watching the smoke float on the light breeze, Rafford felt his entire body relax as his mind began to wander. He thought about when he started this adventure, nearly two years ago. Back then, he was sure that he knew about living in the mountains, but he quickly learned the difference between an occasional mountain camping trip and being a true Adirondacker. Living month-after-month in the mountains made those earlier trips seem more like time spent in a tourist hotel in Lake Placid where you saw the same rugged and rustic scenery but with all the comforts of home. All in all, he decided, the mountains provided their own comforts, and a hot meal over a campfire on a chilly November evening ranked up at the top of his list.

The aroma of baking cornbread brought him back and he lifted the pan from the coals. Baking over a fire is a little tricky, but fresh baked cornbread is worth the risk. He filled his Sierra cup with steaming rice and beans, cut a slab of cornbread and settled back to enjoy his dinner. It was not turkey with all the fixings like back at Deer Run, but it would do just fine.

As he ate, the memories came again, only stronger. Those first days when he had paddled his canoe like a man pursued by demons. Up at dawn each day, he paddled until the sun dropped below the horizon and then seized the first patch of level ground for his camp. Public land or private, it made no difference to him. He was gone, again, early in the morning before anyone would even know he was there. He left no trace; after years of practicing low-impact camping he often left his campsite more pristine than he found it. He made no cook fire, living on beef jerky and trail mix. He knew he could not sustain this pattern for long, but he was in extreme turmoil. Although he paddled until his muscles ached, he slept little, lying awake at night for hours at a time. The hard ground gave his sore muscles little relief, but it was not the pain in his body that kept him awake; it was the deeper pain – the relentless flood of emotions that roared through his every waking hour and disturbed his every thought. What little sleep he found offered no rest. He woke frequently, sometimes shaking violently, but unable to remember the dreams that tormented him. Unable to remember anything, that is, except the one dream that came to him nearly every night. The one he feared when he closed his eyes. The one he recognized as soon as it began. The one that still burned in his eyes even after he awoke.

So he paddled relentlessly through the Fulton Chain to Raquette Lake, then on to Forked Lake and finally to the Raquette river. He spent most of a day portaging around

Buttermilk Falls lining the rapids above and below, before he finally paddled into Long Lake. He explored the Raquette River, and then the Saranac Chain of Lakes. He even did the unnecessary and tedious carry from Weller Pond to Upper Saranac Lake, hoping the carry would drive his demons into submission. It did not. He went on, living on meager rations and punishing his body from sun-up to sundown, hoping for one night, just one night, of deep restful sleep.

Finally, near total exhaustion, he found himself paddling on Follensby Clear Pond, one of his favorite places in the Adirondacks. On instinct, he headed for the lean-to that he knew stood just beyond the narrows of the lake. It was always occupied in the summer months, but this early in the spring, he thought it might be open. He felt an overwhelming sense of relief when he beached the canoe and found the lean-to standing empty.

Before long, he was sitting on the edge of the shelter feeling the soothing warmth of his campfire wash over him, caressing his aching body like a down quilt on a January night. He leaned against his bedroll waiting for the fire to burn down enough for cooking, and fell into a deep, dreamless sleep.

When he awoke, the fire had burned out, the sun was high in the sky and he felt refreshed for the first time in weeks. He took it as a sign – and decided not to paddle that day. Instead, he spent the day feasting on fire-baked cinnamon rolls and freeze-dried eggs with cheese. He emptied his backpack and dry bags, took inventory and reorganized his meager supplies. Living in the Adirondacks for weeks or even months, would not be easy. He decided to stay at the lean-to for a few days, and work out the details.

Rafford shook his head, why am I thinking about those days, now, he wondered.   He broke off another piece of cornbread and wiped the last of the red beans from the bottom of his Sierra cup. Of course, it was the cornbread! That was the reason for remembering those days on Follensby Clear Pond.

That was when he met Warner for the first time – and since then he thought about Warner every time he made cornbread.

On the second day that he spent at the lean-to, he paddled out in the pond to fish for his supper. As he reeled in his third lake trout of the afternoon, the wind came up quickly and the western sky darkened. The storm overtook him in just the few minutes it took for him to paddle back to camp. The skies opened and the rain poured down just as he finished securing his canoe. Dinner would be late.

The rain pounded on the lean-to roof and the trees swayed rhythmically in the wind. He was watching the storm driven waves rise and fall on the lake when he spotted a canoe coming toward him and being tossed violently about by the storm. He put on his rain poncho and ran down to the shoreline, arriving just as the canoe came aground. He grabbed the bow and straddled the gunwales, steadying the boat so its lone occupant could crawl to the front and climb out. The two men dragged the canoe up on the sand and secured it against Rafford's boat, all without speaking. The wind and rain intensified again as they jogged up to the lean-to.

"Well, I didn't see that coming!" the stranger said. "Thanks for your help. I didn't know anyone was here. I hope you don't mind some company."

"Not at all, that's what these lean-tos are for," Rafford answered. "I didn't see any camping gear in your boat – are you just out on a day trip?"

"Sort of, I'm Travis Warner, ENCON Ranger for this area. Today is my day to test pH in these ponds."

"Acid rain," Rafford said knowingly. "Well, you don't need to test the ponds; today, you can test the rain itself! I'm Rafford Brown."

"Well, it's not that easy," said Warner as he shook Rafford's hand.

"I was kidding – you need to track the concentration of pollutants through systematic sampling from the pond. So how does it look?"

"You know about this stuff?"

Rafford smiled, "Yeah, a little, I used to work in environmental science."

"The reading I got on Follensby was 4.8; the pH was slightly higher on Hoel. So it's still pretty bad," Warner answered.

"I'm not surprised. Saddened, but not surprised," Rafford said shaking his head.

The two men sat in silence, watching the rain. The storm showed no signs of easing.

"This looks like it may last a while. It's pretty intense for this time of year," the Ranger said.

Rafford nodded, "It seems more like a summer storm. I remember one August storm when I was camped on Tupper Lake, over on the old IP land. A thunderstorm came up after supper, maybe eight o'clock. Incredible lightning and thunder, you could barely hear yourself curse the storm. Anyway, it went on all night! It finally let up about seven the next morning."

"Well, I don't think this one will be that bad. Still, I may need to stay the night."

"I've got a spare blanket and lake trout for dinner, if we can get a fire going."

"Thanks," Warner said. "I always carry a bedroll in my day pack. The trout sounds good – you didn't go over your limit, did you?"

Rafford laughed, "No, the storm came up before I could. It will be nice to have company for a change."

"How long have you been here?"

"I got here two days ago, but I'm about 10 days into the trip."

The two men talked easily for the next half-hour, mostly about the times they had spent in the Adirondacks. The winds finally eased, but the rain showed no sign of letting up.

"Well, I guess it's time to test my old Boy Scout skills, and see if I can start a fire in the rain. I stashed some dry kindling under the lean-to that should get us started."

Warner offered, "I have some birch bark strips in my pack, and an old tarp in the canoe. Maybe if we cover part of the fire ring..."

The two men worked quickly, calling on years of outdoor experience. They tied the tarp to the beam under the front of the lean-to roof and the opposite side to a taut line strung between two trees. They were careful to angle the tarp so the rain would run off and the smoke from the fire would draft away from the lean-to. The birch bark and dry kindling soon ignited some larger pieces that were wet on the outside but dry enough inside to burn. In less than an hour, they were roasting trout over a bed of coals.

"Fish on a stick, the height of Adirondack cuisine!" Warner said with a chuckle.

Rafford placed some left over corn bread wrapped in foil right into the coals, "All we need now, is a cold beer," he said.

Warner replied, "Sorry, cold beer is one thing I don't have in my pack. But I do have a bottle of ginger schnapps for an after dinner drink!"

"Ranger Warner, you are full of surprises! The schnapps – is that standard issue for Rangers these days?"

"Rangers, like Boy Scouts, must always be prepared," Warner said with a smile.

The fish and cornbread disappeared quickly. As Warner rummaged through his pack for the bottle of schnapps, Rafford wiped out his enamel coffee mug and his Sierra Cup. The schnapps was spicy on his tongue and burned his throat as he swallowed. Warner poured a second shot for each of them, and this one went down much smoother.

"The more you drink, the smoother it gets," Warner said, as he poured yet another for each of them.

By the time the bottle was half-empty, the rain had stopped and stars began to appear through the thinning clouds. There was no moon, so the starlight shone brilliantly against the black night sky.

"Maybe it's the schnapps, but I don't think there is a more beautiful place on earth," Rafford said.

"It's not the schnapps," Warner replied. "Drunk or sober, there is no place like the Adirondacks. I've lived here all my life and the mountains, the lakes, the forests – they all just fit together perfectly, like an intricate jigsaw puzzle. Cover it all with a canopy of stars like this – well, there is nowhere else I'd rather be."

Rafford nodded in agreement, "The first time I came to the Adirondacks, it felt like I was coming home. I'd never been here before, never even heard much of the Adirondacks, but that first time it was all so familiar, so right, I didn't want to leave. We moved around a lot, when I was a kid, so no one place ever really felt like home. I learned how to adjust, how to fit-in wherever we were, but I always felt like the outsider, a visitor in someone else's house. But here, in the mountains, it is different; I feel like I belong here."

Rafford looked around, self-consciously. "Sorry. I don't usually go on like that. It must be the schnapps."

Warner did not say anything. Rafford looked closer and saw that the Ranger had fallen asleep, his head resting against the side of the lean-to.

"Warner!" Rafford said aloud, shook his head, and laughed. Why did I think about Warner now? It's been nearly two years since that day on Follensby Clear Pond, and I have not seen him since last year when he told me about that winter job in Tupper Lake. So, why remember that day, now? Yup, it must be the cornbread; Warner always loved his cornbread.

He and Warner had seen each other regularly during Rafford's first year in the mountains. Although, Rafford moved camp every couple of weeks, Warner always seemed to know where to find him. When he came to visit, he always brought a bottle of schnapps for after dinner. Sometimes they talked deep into the night and other times they just enjoyed the quiet that surrounded them. Either way, their love of the Adirondacks built a solid bond between them.

Rafford finished his dinner, then cleaned up quickly and secured camp for the night. By sunset, he had neatly stacked the firewood, hung the bear bag high in a tree and laid out his bedroll. He wrote his daily entry in his trail journal by the faint glow of the fire. He noted his location, his special meal and his memories of Warner. He went to bed early, expecting the next day would be a busy one.

Early the next morning, Rafford bushwhacked a trail across the base of Hart Mountain. He moved quickly, carrying only a daypack. Picking his way through the underbrush he moved steadily westward and upward, cutting a diagonal line across the slope. He did not need to get to the top of the mountain, just high enough to gain a vantage point with a clear view. Every few minutes he paused to check his compass – just to be sure he could find his way back to camp, even in the dark.

He found a level ridgeline about a third of the way up the side of Hart Mountain and followed it until he saw Abigail's fence in the distance below. He moved cautiously from this point forward, especially where the ridgeline separated from the forest. He finally found a spot that offered a clear view but one that was secreted by a cluster of fir trees and a downed paper birch. He settled in, careful to remain hidden from view, took the binoculars from his pack and waited. He did not have to wait long.

Below him on the gun club side of the fence, he saw them: four ATVs roaring two-by-two along a super-highway of a trail. The riders, all in full camouflage, carried rifles slung over their shoulders. Out of the corner of his eye, Rafford saw a flash of movement. Below him, on the upslope of the mountain, he spotted the same pregnant doe that he and Amos had seen before. She moved clumsily through the brush, spooked by the noise, and then disappeared beneath a large spruce tree. Rafford heard the ATVs stop and looked quickly back to the hunters who sat only a hundred yards from where he perched. They were unshouldering their guns, but looking away from where he had seen the doe. It was only then that he saw yet another ATV moving down the mountain driven by a man that he recognized, even from this distance, as George Harder. The ATV zigzagged through the underbrush, with repeated changes of direction, but moving steadily toward the other four men. Harder appeared to be concentrating on something in the brush. Then Rafford saw them – a flock of wild turkeys, 4 adults and a collection of young ones too quick for Rafford to count. Harder was herding them, driving them from state owned land directly toward the men who waited below.

The ambush was unleashed with abandon. The hunters fired repeatedly into the brush where the turkeys cowered. One bird rose briefly above the slaughter, frantically flapping its wings, only to crash down again in a flurry of gunfire and feathers. When the guns fell silent, nothing moved in the brush.

The men whooped and hollered; one even fired his rifle into the air, as Harder rode in among them. Harder stepped off his ATV and tromped through the brush gathering their trophies. He piled the four adults into the carrier on the back of his four-wheeler, but he left the young ones where they fell. One of the hunters took a long draw on a liquor bottle, and then passed it around. Harder waived off the bottle and motioned for them to leave. The four men headed back down the wide trail.

Harder remained, looking around the forest as if he sensed something. His eyes scanned the fence line in both directions as he searched the woods on Abigail's land. He drove the ATV slowly following the fence line and looking closely at the ground. At one point, he dismounted and knelt down to touch the snow. Rafford guessed that he had found animal tracks, and he hoped that Harder would not discover the pregnant doe.

Harder took one more look around, and then started up the ATV. He threw a rope around one of the fence posts and then turned away from the fence. When he gunned the engine, the ATV jumped forward, snapping the post in half. He moved about 15 feet down the line and snapped another post, and then another, before finally roaring off down the same trail that the others had taken.

Rafford remained hidden for another 20 minutes, in case they returned. He watched the brush wondering if any of the young turkeys had survived, but he saw nothing. He watched for the doe, too, but she did not reappear.

Finally, when he felt sure the hunters had gone, he carefully retraced his steps along the hillside and crossed the fence line back to Abigail's property. He was not sure what he would do, but he was determined that Harder had to be stopped.

❧❧

Chapter Nine

Abigail went to the window repeatedly on Saturday afternoon. She pretended to be checking on the snow that had been falling since daybreak but, in truth, she was looking for sign of Rafford's return. It was not until after she and Carolyn had finished washing the supper dishes that she saw light in the tack room window. Standing in the open doorway, she smelled the sweet smoke from the woodstove. Rafford had returned.

"Still snowing, Mom?" Carolyn asked.

"Yes, but there looks to be only six or seven inches on the ground. If it stops soon, you will be able to get out tomorrow," Abigail replied.

"The radio says the storm is winding down, so we'll see."

"It's November and it's snowing in the Adirondacks – no surprise," Abigail chuckled. Then after a moment she added, "Rafford's back."

Carolyn shrugged, "So, I guess that means you can stop checking on the snow, every five minutes. Look, I still don't know why you feel so strongly about him, but I'll try to talk to him in the morning, you know, to smooth things over. Right now, I'm going upstairs to finish packing and then I'm going to bed. I need to get an early start in the morning, just in case the weather doesn't cooperate. "

Tyler sat on one end of the sofa with Smokey's head resting on his feet. He looked up from his comic book and said, "Wake me up before you go tomorrow, Mom."

"Absolutely. You may have to help shovel snow so I can get to the airport", Carolyn replied with a smile.

"Yeah, it would be a shame if you missed your plane and couldn't go to Texas."

"All right, wise guy, we have been through this a million times. I will only be gone for three weeks and I'll call you every night. You're going to have a great time here with Grandma."

Tyler did not answer; he just nodded slowly and kept his eyes downcast. Abigail could see that he was not happy about staying behind with her, and frankly, she was not sure what she would do to entertain him for the next three weeks.

"Tyler, I've been thinking," she said. "There is a lot of work to do around this old place and I just don't have time to do everything myself. While you are here, would you do a big favor for me and take care of Smokey? Sometimes I get so busy, I don't have time for him and he feels neglected. I wouldn't have to worry about him, though, if I knew that you would feed him and take him outside, and maybe even play with him once in a while. He's old, but he still likes to play, sometimes. Would you do that for me? I would really appreciate it."

Tyler looked at the dog and scratched him behind the ears. "I guess so. Could he sleep in my room?"

"That's up to Smokey," she said. "He usually makes the rounds of the house at night, but if you leave your door open, I bet he will sleep with you, at least part of the night."

She looked for signs of enthusiasm from Tyler, but the boy just looked at the dog, as though he was considering her proposition. He had worn the same expression on his face since they arrived. It was not a look of sadness in his eyes but more a vacant look, a detached gaze that appeared very out-of-place on a ten-year-old boy.

"So what do you say?" she asked breezily.

"Okay, Grandma, I'll take care of him."

Later that night, as Abigail was on her way to bed, she peeked into Tyler's room, and saw Smokey sleeping soundly on the foot of the bed. She smiled and mumbled to herself, "What is it about little boys and dogs?"

Tyler woke early in the morning with Smokey nuzzling his face. He lay in bed for a few moments listening to the quiet house. Smokey nudged him, again, and he rolled out of bed and quietly dressed himself.

Downstairs, in the mudroom, he put on his boots, winter coat and hat. Smokey stood patiently by the door, wagging his tail and glancing first at Tyler then at the closed door.

The sun dangled low in the gray November sky as they stepped out onto the porch. Tyler followed Smokey down the steps but, for a moment, he was blinded by a flash of sunlight reflecting off the snow. When his eyes readjusted, he saw Smokey running straight toward Rafford who was shoveling a path from the barn toward the house.

"Good morning!" Rafford said. "You're up early."

"Good morning," Tyler said politely, but without enthusiasm.

"I'm Rafford Brown, I work for Abi –" he stopped. "I work for your Grandmother. I guess we didn't really get introduced the other day."

"My mother said you were gone and that you wouldn't come back."

"Is that so? What did your Grandmother say? Did she see my note?"

"I don't know," Tyler mumbled as he looked down at his boots and fiddled with his gloves.

"After I finish shoveling this walkway, I'm going to plow the driveway. I could use a hand, would you help me?" Rafford asked.

"I don't know – what do you want me to do?"

"There's another snow shovel up there on the porch. You can start by clearing the front steps."

When they had finished the walkway, Rafford led Tyler out to the barn, and started up the old Kubota tractor. Tyler was fascinated by the many handles and levers used to drive the tractor and manipulate the plow. He stayed a few steps behind Rafford, following his every move as he walked around the tractor checking the bolts and connecting rods. Tyler put his hands over his ears trying to block out the growling noise of the tractor engine that reverberated off the barn walls. When Rafford had finished his inspection, he reached below the steering wheel for the choke and backed it off allowing the engine to settle into a much quieter idling rhythm.

Rafford motioned to Tyler to come closer, and then he leaned near to Tyler's ear and said, "You see all those levers? The big one with the red knob shifts the transmission. The other three control the height and angle of the snowplow blade. It's a lot for one person to do and still be able to steer the tractor. So, what I need you to do is steer the tractor for me, while I do the rest. Can you do that?"

The boy looked down at his feet, shook his head side-to-side, and said very quietly, "I can't; I don't know how to steer a tractor."

Rafford could not hear what he said, but he could tell the boy was afraid. "Tyler, it's very easy – I'll show you what to do."

Tyler kept looking at his feet and did not respond.

"Tyler – look at me," Rafford had to lift the boy's chin to see his eyes. "You don't have to do this, but it would really be a big help. It's up to you, do you want to give it a try?"

The boy shrugged his shoulders and then nodded his head tentatively.

Inside the house, Abigail was making breakfast when she heard Smokey scratching at the mudroom door. Smokey never liked the noise of the tractor, and whenever it was in use, he always ran back to the house. She opened the door to let him in and gasped aloud when she saw Tyler sitting behind the wheel of the tractor as it pushed a large pile of snow away from the livestock pen.

"Carolyn! Come down here; you've got to see this!" she called.

When Carolyn saw the boy behind the wheel, she panicked, pushed open the door and started to call out, but Abigail cut her off.

"No! Carolyn wait," Abigail said quickly. "He's all right. Rafford is right there with him. See?"

Carolyn stopped and looked closer. She saw Rafford, but what she noticed more than anything was the look of pure joy on Tyler's face.

Just then, the boy looked toward the house and waved, "Mom! Look!"

As she waved back, she saw Rafford say something to the boy. Tyler quickly nodded, and then put both hands back on the wheel and turned his eyes back to the front of the tractor.

"Looks like Tyler and Rafford are off to a good start," Abigail said and then turned back to the kitchen before Carolyn could answer.

They had plowed only half of the long driveway when Abigail called them to breakfast. Tyler came running, bubbling over with excitement.

"Mom, did you see? I was driving the Cumona! It's loud, but boy is it powerful! It just pushes the snow right out of the way! Rafford – uh, Mr. Brown – is gonna teach me how to shift gears and run the plow, too! Did you see me, Grandma?"

"Slow down," Carolyn said. "We saw you. Weren't you scared? I mean, you never did anything like that before."

"No, I wasn't scared. It's just a tractor – besides Rafford told me what to do. He knows all about that old Cumona!!"

"Kubota, Ty, Kubota," Carolyn corrected.

"Yeah, Kubota. Anyway, I can't stop to eat right now. We have to finish the driveway."

As he turned to go back outside, Abigail stopped him, "Wait – here take this with you." She rolled up a sausage link in one of his favorite blueberry pancakes and handed it to him.

"Thanks, Grandma. Can I have one for Rafford, too?" he asked. He turned to his mother, "Mom, is it okay to not to call him Mr. Brown? He said to call him Rafford..."

"I guess so, if he said it was okay."

By the time Carolyn finished her reply, the boy was out the door on the run toward the driveway.

Carolyn said, "I've never seen him like this. Usually, he is very timid around strangers, especially men. Maybe it's the tractor..."

Abigail smiled and shook her head, but said nothing.

Rafford and Tyler finished clearing the driveway. Rafford had just shut down the tractor when Carolyn walked into the barn. The boy saw her first, jumped down from the tractor and ran over to her.

"Come, here, Mom, I'll show you how the snow plow works. Come on!"

"I don't have time right now, Ty. I have to go to the airport. My suitcase is on the porch. Would you put it in the car for me, please?"

After Tyler left, Carolyn walked over to where Rafford was wiping down the plow cables. "I noticed the broken headlight on my car was replaced. Did you do that?"

Rafford nodded, "I tried to get a new lens for the turn signal but they had to order it. It should be here when you get back from your trip."

"Thank you. Mr. Brown," she said. "I want to apologize for my outburst the other day."

"No apology, needed. "

"No – I want to explain. My mother had told me about you, but somehow I just wasn't prepared to see you standing there. Whenever, I come back here, I can't help but think about my father – everything about this place reminds me of him. And, well, when I saw you wearing that barn coat of his, it was..." Carolyn could not finish the sentence. She was surprised and embarrassed that her eyes welled-up.

"Like I said, no apology needed. I didn't mean to offend you or anybody. Your mother is one of the sweetest people I have ever known. She gave me those clothes to wear and made me feel so much at home here that I just didn't think. I'm the one who should apologize," Rafford said.

"I must tell you that I was worried when my mother told me that she had a man living here with her for the winter. She knew so little about you and I just assumed the worst. Anyway, having you here seems to be good for her."

Before Rafford could reply, she continued, "Now about the tractor; it worked out okay today, Ty didn't get hurt, but please don't ever do anything like that again. Tyler's a good boy, but he's not used to being around men and machines and such. So please don't push him to do things that he is not ready to do – I mean, he is only ten years old. If he gets hurt, or if anything bad happens to him while I am gone, I will hold you personally responsible."

"Now, wait a minute, I didn't do anything to put him in danger. I was right there the whole time, he was perfectly safe."

"Well, don't ever do it again! I don't think it was safe and as his mother, I have the final word."

"Having the final word seems to be a trait of Sherwood women," Rafford muttered under his breath.

"What was that," Carolyn asked?

"Nothing. I just thought driving the tractor would take his mind off being stuck here for the next few weeks."

"Oh, so you don't approve of my trip to Texas, either! Look, I know what is best for my son and me, and, besides, it is only for three weeks. So I will thank you to keep your snap judgments to yourself!"

Abigail appeared in the doorway and said, "It seems to me the only snap judgments around here are coming from you, Carolyn."

"Mother – "

"Don't Mother, me. I think you had better leave before you say any more stupid things. Besides, you have a plane to catch. Remember, you are not leaving Tyler with Rafford, you are leaving him with me, and I know a thing or two about raising children."

≪⫷ ⫸≫

Chapter Ten

Rafford and Abigail quickly settled back into their routine after Carolyn left. For the first few days Tyler was like a shadow on a late fall afternoon: there, but nearly invisible. Although Abigail tried repeatedly to draw him out, Tyler seemed to fade into the background.. He would do whatever she asked, quickly, quietly, but with little enthusiasm.

"I don't know what to do," Abigail said to Rafford one night after Tyler had gone to bed. "Nothing seems to interest him. It's as though he is treading water, trying not to make waves. I thought that after a few days he would relax and feel at home here. Now, I just don't know."

"Maybe he just needs a little more time," Rafford replied, without much conviction.

"Rafford," she said gently, "maybe if he spent a little more time with you. He was so excited about the tractor. I've noticed him watching you, working around the barn. He keeps his distance, but he's always watching. You know, he's never really been around men. It might do him good to work with you. At least, he might learn a few things."

Rafford did not answer right away, but finally spoke, "I don't know if that's a good idea. What about Carolyn? We didn't get off to a very good start and she was pretty clear..."

Abigail interrupted, "I love my daughter, but she can be nigh on to impossible when it comes to Tyler."

"I've seen it first hand, remember?" he replied. "But I don't blame her. She is just trying to be a good mother. Raising a boy, alone, must be tough, especially these days. It's hard on Tyler, but it's got to be hard on Carolyn, too."

"I know," said Abigail. "But every time I look at Tyler I see my boy Richie, at his age. I remember how he followed his dad around, trying to be like him. He learned by imitating everything that Roger did. How is Tyler going to learn how to be a man?"

"He's only ten, Abigail," Rafford chuckled. "He's got time. Besides, I'm not exactly a role model for little boys. I'm nearly thirty-five years old, and until I came here, I was living in a tent! Little boys look up to heroes like astronauts or athletes, not guys like me."

"I'm not asking you to be his hero or his father; just to spend a little time with him. See what happens; I think you would be good for him."

"I need to think it over, okay?"

Abigail nodded, then said, "Don't forget, we are going to look for a Christmas tree tomorrow. Maybe we can talk more then?"

"Let's see what happens," Rafford said.

Early the next morning, after breakfast and the morning chores, Abigail, Tyler and Rafford set out in search of Abigail's perfect Christmas tree. Abigail was bubbling over with enthusiasm as they drove the pickup truck along the rutted fire road.

"What a beautiful day!" she said. "Just enough snow on the ground to make it feel like Christmas. I'm so glad you two are here. Last year I had to get crotchety old Amos Kreal to cut down my tree. Amos may look like Santa Claus but the resemblance is purely coincidental. He griped and complained the whole time!"

"Grandma, it's not Christmas yet, why are you so excited?" Tyler asked.

"Christmas will be here before you know it. Besides, getting ready for Christmas is almost as good as Christmas itself! And today is the official first day of 'getting-ready-for-Christmas!'"

Rafford tried to stifle his laughter, but when Tyler looked at him, questioningly, he could not hold it in. They both laughed long and loud while Abigail pretended to be offended.

When they came to the end of the road, Rafford parked the truck. He pulled his daypack and hiking staff from the pickup bed, picked out an open trail, and set off into the woods. He led them gradually away from the fence line, hoping to avoid any contact with the men from the gun club. The three walked without speaking for about ten minutes, the only sound coming from their boots crunching through the icy crust on the snow. Then abruptly, Rafford stopped and knelt down on one knee.

Tyler came up beside him trying to see what Rafford was looking at, "What are you doing?"

Rafford pointed to a line of marks in the snow, "What do you think these marks are?"

The boy knelt beside him and looked at a line of marks - each one looking like a letter Y stamped clearly in the fresh snow.

"Are they animal tracks?"

"Very good" Rafford nodded. "A wild turkey, I think. You can tell from this back line. This is a good day for finding animal tracks because of the fresh snow. Why don't you walk in front, for a while and see what you find?"

"I can't; I don't know which way to go."

"Sure you can – we're just out for a walk in the woods. Just keep moving forward and watch out for low branches."

"But what if we get lost?"

"Look behind us," Rafford replied.

The boy looked back and saw the wide trail their boots had marked in the snow.

"All we have to do is follow our own trail back to the truck. Besides, your Grandma knows every inch of these woods, so she won't let us get lost."

Reluctantly, Tyler set off, walking slowly at first, stopping frequently to look closer at marks in the snow. After a few minutes, he pointed excitedly, and shouted, "Look!"

"Not so loud," Rafford whispered. "When you see tracks the animal may still be close by."

All three of them knelt to look at the line of paw prints that Tyler had found.

"What do you think they are, Tyler?"

"I don't know," the boy said quickly.

"Well, look at them and try to imagine what kind of animal might make a track like that. Remember how the turkey tracks we found were made of thin lines? Bird tracks look like that because of the shape of their feet. What kind of foot would make a track like this?"

"I don't know – it kind of looks like a dog's paw print."

"Why?" asked Rafford.

"Because of the big round mark and the smaller round ones next to it that look like toes."

"Very good. Many animals leave paw prints that have 'toes', but I think you're right. This looks like a dog's paw print. When you see a paw print like this in the woods, it might be from a dog or from another animal like a dog. Maybe a coyote or –"

"Or a wolf!" Tyler exclaimed.

Rafford smiled, "Well, it might be a wolf, but wolves are very rare in the Adirondacks and a wolf print would probably be bigger than these. My guess is that you have found coyote tracks. Good work!"

"Let's keep going and see what else we can find."

Abigail spoke up, "Yes, let's go on. Maybe we will even find a Christmas tree!"

For the next half-hour, they walked through the woods, looking for tracks and evaluating and rejecting more than a dozen trees until finally, Abigail announced, "This is it! This tree will be perfect."

Rafford and Tyler walked around the tree, two full circles, before giving her their approval. It was a balsam, nearly eight feet tall, with lush green needles.

"How are we gonna cut it down?" Tyler asked. "We don't have an ax or anything."

"Oh, we won't cut it today, it's too soon. We will mark it today so you and Rafford can find it again when you come back in a couple of weeks to cut it down. That way it will stay nice and fresh through the holidays."

Abigail pulled a large handful of fabric strips from the pocket of her coat and handed some strips to each of them. The sweet smell of balsam filled the air as they tied the fabric in knots and bows all over the tree.

When they had finished, Rafford brushed the snow from a large boulder nearby, and set his daypack on the flat top. From the pack, he produced bananas, graham crackers with peanut butter and his own trail mix of homemade granola, nuts, raisins and dried cranberries. As they snacked, Tyler picked up Rafford's walking stick and fingered the carvings and cord wrappings that decorated it.

"Did you carve these animals?" he asked.

Rafford nodded, "Yes, I did. I've had that stick a long time, and every so often, sitting by the campfire at night, I add another decoration, but I'm not very good at it."

"Why do you carry it?"

"Sometimes it comes in handy – when the trail is difficult, or when you need to reach something. Once I used it to help a friend keep from losing his backpack over a waterfall. Another time, it propped up my rain tarp and kept me dry in a storm. Mostly, I just like the way it feels to have a walking stick along on a hike. If you want to see what I mean, I noticed some good sticks over there by that downed tree. Why don't you pick one out and pick out one for your Grandmother – just for the walk back. Try to find ones that are pretty straight and not rotted."

Tyler very deliberately examined several sticks, before selecting two. Rafford quickly trimmed the sticks with the Buck knife that he always carried on his belt.

When they were ready to start the walk back to the truck Rafford spoke to the boy, "Tyler, I was wondering if you would like to spend some time each day working with me. I have a lot to do and I could use some help. Besides, it would be nice to have someone to talk to besides the chickens. What do you think?"

Tyler looked at his boots, "I don't know how to do much."

"I can show you how to do things; we'd work together. You did real well with the tractor, so I know you can learn."

The boy did not answer so Abigail spoke up, "Tyler, why don't you think about it while we hike back. If you don't want to work with Rafford, that is okay. But think about it."

Tyler nodded, still looking down as he scuffed the snow with the toe of his boot.

On the way back to the truck, Tyler once again took the lead and scanned the snow for animal tracks. When they had walked about fifteen minutes, their trail crossed a line of hoof prints that Rafford immediately recognized as deer tracks. The tracks headed straight toward the fence line and the gun club's land.

"What kind of tracks are these?" Tyler asked.

"Deer," Rafford answered.

"Why didn't we see them before, when we walked through here?" the boy asked.

"These are fresh tracks, probably not more than a few minutes old. See how clear and sharp the marks are? The snow hasn't melted at all, not even these little clumps that fell from the deer's hooves as she walked through. She must have been here just a few minutes ago."

"How do you know it's a she?" he asked.

"Good question - I don't," Rafford lied.

He was sure that these tracks were from the pregnant doe that he and Amos had spotted a few days ago. Now, she was too close to the gun club for her own good.

"Where is it? Can we see it?" Tyler asked excitedly.

Abigail shook her head and started to speak, but Rafford interrupted.

"Maybe we can; let's give it a try. We'll have to be very quiet. If she knows we are following her she will probably head deeper into the woods." Rafford nodded toward the woods and away from the gun club fence line. Abigail understood what he meant; maybe they could turn the deer away from danger, and back toward State land.

Rafford led the way, circling well to the north of the deer's tracks, staying downwind. They moved slowly and quietly, stopping frequently to look for the deer. Rafford knew they were close to where he and Amos had first seen the doe, and he guessed that she must have a nesting spot nearby.

They were crouched behind a snowdrift when Rafford spotted the doe in front of them, just beyond a clearing in the woods. He motioned to Abigail and Tyler to stay still and then pointed in the direction of the deer. For two or three minutes, they watched, barely breathing, afraid to make a sound. Suddenly the doe raised her head and with amazing quickness leaped to one side. In two swift steps, she disappeared into the woods, headed safely away from the fence line.

Tyler was impressed. All the way back to the truck, he searched constantly for animal tracks and scanned the woods for deer.

When Tyler was far enough ahead that he could not hear her, Abigail said "Rafford, that doe was pregnant. "

Rafford nodded, "I saw her when Amos and I were mending the fence a couple of weeks ago. I've never heard of a fawn being born this time of year, have you?"

"No – the poor thing won't stand much of a chance. Maybe we should try to keep an eye on her. She's probably got a nesting spot picked out around here."

"OK – I'll come back in a couple of days and see if I can track her down," Rafford agreed.

"One thing, Rafford – don't tell Tyler about the fawn. I doubt that this story will have a happy ending."

۞

Chapter Eleven

R afford tried to warn Amos when he arrived for breakfast the next day, but Abigail got to him first and let him know exactly what she thought about them keeping the pregnant doe a secret. When she had finished with her half-serious rant, Abigail assigned him to help Rafford keep an eye on the doe over the coming days.

"I told you she'd have us playing wet nurse to that doe," Amos said to Rafford when Abigail was safely out of earshot.

Rafford replied with a knowing smile, "Truthfully, I planned to look after the doe, even without Abigail's orders. I'm curious about her and her fawn, but even more, I'm determined to keep George Harder and his gun club commandos away from her. I won't let them poach yet another deer – especially this deer – for display on their antler pole."

Abigail returned to the kitchen and Amos quickly changed the subject, "Gonna snow, tonight – big storm –looks like winter is here early this year."

"I heard the forecast," she answered. "It's too early for a Nor'easter but they sound pretty sure. Rafford, I think you'll find some snowshoes up in the hayloft. Why don't you see if there is a pair that will fit you and maybe a smaller pair for

Tyler? If you don't need them tonight, you probably will need them soon."

"I'll look for them right after Amos and I mend that break in the livestock pen."

"Maybe, Amos could get your supplies together. I'd like to talk to you, alone, for a moment."

Amos didn't wait to be told a second time. He grabbed his cap and a second banana muffin, and headed for the back door.

Abigail turned to Rafford, "I've been thinking about you sleeping in that tack room with winter getting serious. It's got to be cold and drafty, especially in a storm. Maybe you should move into the house; there's a guest room upstairs that's never used."

Rafford began shaking his head as soon as she mentioned moving, "No – thank you, Abigail. I am comfortable in the tack room – that old wood stove keeps out the cold, just fine. You already treat me like a member of the family, and I'm grateful for that, but it wouldn't be right for me to move into the house. Thanks, anyway, but I'll stay in the tack room."

"If its Carolyn, you're worried about..."

Rafford interrupted her, "It's not Carolyn. I just feel better having my own place. But thanks for the kind offer."

Amos and Rafford had just finished repairing the livestock pen, when Tyler joined them in the barn. "I thought it over, and I would like to work with you," he said to Rafford.

"Does this mean I'm out of a job?" Amos asked suppressing a smile.

"No, Amos," Rafford replied, "but it does mean that you had better watch your step, because you can be replaced!"

The two men laughed at Rafford's remark, but Tyler did not join in. Rafford noticed that the boy seemed unsure of Amos Kreal. Abigail had mentioned that Tyler had been around Amos once or twice before, when he was younger, but that he had always been afraid of the old man.

The three of them climbed up the ladder into the barn attic. They walked past piles of hay bales neatly stacked in the loft and entered the enclosed storage area at the far end of the barn. On one side stood stacks of boxes and crates, all neatly labeled and sealed. Some of the labels read "Roger Sherwood" and held the things that Abigail had packed up after he died but could not bear to let go. Others boxes had Carolyn's name on them, and were filled the usual detritus left behind when children move away from home. On the opposite side of the storage area, Rafford noticed two large shapeless mounds covered with canvas tarps. Inside the chicken wire barrier that separated the storage area from the rest of the loft, several sets of snowshoes and worn wooden cross-country skis in assorted sizes hung on the wall with at least a dozen bamboo ski poles.

Rafford and Amos sorted through the snowshoes and quickly found a pair that fit Tyler perfectly. The wooden snowshoes were beaver-tail design, but not quite as wide as most, and that would make them easier for Tyler to handle.

"The size is perfect," Amos said as they slipped Tyler's foot into the binding. "I'll have to resize the binding and replace a couple of straps, but these will do fine. Have you ever worn snowshoes, Tyler?"

The boy shook his head, no.

"Well, you'll learn. It really is not hard, once you learn how to keep your feet from banging into one another," Amos laughed at the thought.

Rafford found a solid pair of bamboo ski poles for the boy, "I can cut these down a bit, so they are just your size. Now, let's see if we can find a pair of snowshoes to fit me."

While Rafford and Amos examined the snowshoes, Tyler wandered around the attic. Curious, he peeled back the tarp from one of the piles and uncovered an ornate wooden dogsled.

"Wow!" Tyler exclaimed, causing Rafford and Amos to turn toward him.

"Wow, is right," echoed Rafford as he forgot about the snowshoes and walked over to the sled. "This must be Roger's handiwork; the sleek lines and these hand-carved maple dowels here on the frame!   Look how the runners bend up in front. He must have steamed and laminated thirty pieces of wood to get that shape!"

"Yep, that's Roger's work, all right," Amos confirmed. "Everything, except those runners.   I made those, myself. Roger didn't have the patience for steam work. I was a cooper in my early days in the logging camps. Not bad work, if I do say so myself."

"Amos, you are full of surprises," Rafford said while shaking his head. "I had no idea you could do this kind of work."

"Tyler, this dogsled was your Grandpa's pride and joy," Amos said. "He could make it fly, barely skimming across the top of the snow, the way a flat stone skims across a still pond! Years ago, he had the fastest four-dog team in the mountains! He even raced them a couple of times up on the ice at Lake Placid. "

"Did he win?" Tyler asked.

"You bet he did!" the old man replied. "Left the others so far behind they had to send out a search party to lead them in!"

"Amos," Rafford said purposefully.

"Well, they almost did. Say, don't let old Smokey see this sled. He always got so excited whenever Roger would let him work the sled – I guess it's born in some dogs."

"Do you think he would still be able to pull it?" Tyler asked excitedly.

"I imagine so, although Roger used to work him in tandem with another dog. But I bet old Smoke could pull it around the yard a couple of times!"

"If you got Smokey to pull it, could I have a ride in the sled sometime?" the boy asked Amos.

"I don't think Smokey could pull us both. I'd have to teach you how to drive the sled, yourself."

"No," Tyler said quickly, "that's OK. I couldn't do that."

"Of course, you could," Amos said emphatically. "Driving a dogsled is basically just holding on tight, anyway – especially with an old experienced sled-dog like Smokey in the harness."

Rafford had been examining the sled and interrupted, "It doesn't matter, anyway. This sled won't pull, no matter who's driving. It needs a lot of work, this runner has totally broken free and there are cracks along the bottom of the frame. Besides, it's too good-looking to take chances."

"Oh, don't be ridiculous! I made those runners, so I can surely fix them. And those cracks in the frame have been there since the time Roger christened Suicide Hill. We didn't build this sled to be beautiful or to be covered up in an old barn attic! We built it to run, and if Roger were here, he'd be the first to say so!" Amos turned to Tyler, "So, what do you say, boy? Shall we spruce her up and give Smokey another chance to run?"

Tyler looked at the sled, and then at Rafford. Finally, he turned to Amos and nodded, "Okay."

For the next three days, Amos arrived at Deer Run in time to have breakfast with Tyler. When Rafford had finished his morning chores, the three of them worked on the sled, together. Just as Amos had promised, it was soon ready to run. The leather dog harness had long since rotted, so while Tyler and Rafford gave the sled a fresh coat of spar varnish, Amos made a new one-dog rig out of leather strips and rope. It would not be strong enough for a long trip, but it would suffice for Tyler's lessons.

Smokey watched every move they made with explosive enthusiasm. From the moment the sled appeared in the barn, the old dog was beside himself. He bounded around the sled, his tail wagging, while he barked and whined simultaneously, in anticipation.

When the sled was finally ready, Abigail and Rafford watched Amos buckle Smokey into the harness. Then Amos stood between the runners at the back of the sled, took a firm grip, and called out to Smokey, "Hup!"

Instantly, the dog bolted forward kicking up a spray of snow from his back paws. His powerful start surprised Amos and the old man stumbled forward as the dog nearly jerked the sled out of his hands. Two quick steps later, Amos jumped onto the runners and let Smokey feel his full weight. Smokey slowed a little, but he dug his paws deeper into the snow and kept moving forward. Amos skillfully steered the sled in a large oval circling the yard.

As they returned to the front of the barn, he called to the dog, "Whoa, Smokey", and they slid to a stop. The dog's sides were heaving and his tongue flicked the top of the snow, but his tail never stopped wagging.

"Well, I don't know about you, Amos" laughed Abigail, "but Smokey still has the gift. I had forgotten how much he loved to run with that sled."

Amos did not answer, but his face beamed. He called Tyler over to the sled, and in only a few minutes, Tyler was steering the sled as Amos led Smokey by the harness. An hour later, Tyler drove the sled solo, once around the yard.

"That's enough for today," Amos called. "Smokey isn't ready for this. Even though he wants to pull, we have to go slowly."

Together, they put the sled safely away in the barn. Tyler took Smokey back to the house for food and water, and Amos headed for his truck.

"Amos," Abigail called, "dinner will be ready in 10 minutes."

"Is that an invitation?" he answered.

Rafford came up beside him, "Be careful, Amos, remember you want to stay on her good side!"

"Thanks, Abigail," Amos called, "but I can't stay tonight. I got things to do."

"Suit yourself."

Rafford chuckled, "I think that means 'thank you for what you have done for Tyler'. This dog sled has been really good for him."

Amos just smiled, "It's been good for me, too. But if I don't go home and rest these old bones, I'll never be able to keep up with our boy tomorrow!"

Tyler chattered non-stop, all through dinner, while Abigail and Rafford just listened. They both were amazed at the difference in his attitude. The tentative ill at ease little boy, of a few days ago, was gone, and the new Tyler was something to behold.

Late that night, Rafford awoke with a start and then sat up in bed, listening. A moment later, he heard the sound again -- and this time he was sure he heard gunfire coming from the direction of Hart Mountain. He quickly pulled on his boots and a woolen shirt and ran to the barn. He scaled the ladder to the hayloft and jogged to the window at the north end. The new moon and thick cloud cover made the night especially dark. Looking toward Hart Mountain, he saw the headlights of several snowmobiles flaring through the blackness like laser beams in a science fiction movie. Rafford counted at least six lights moving in a serpentine pattern. It was impossible to be sure from this distance, but it looked like the snowmobiles were on Abigail's side of the fence line. Then the lights stopped moving and, as if on signal, they all went dark. Only then did he notice the single light weaving down the side of Hart Mountain toward the place where the other snowmobiles waited. That high up on Hart Mountain had to be State land, Rafford thought; Abigail's property ended at the base of the mountain. He watched the lone rider, sure that it was George Harder, and pictured him driving some poor animal toward the waiting hunters. Moments later, the six snowmobile lights flashed on again and the night was shattered by another volley of gunfire.

Then it was over. The snowmobiles roared off toward the Northwest – a direction that would lead them back to Black Stag Gun Club property. Rafford watched for a few more minutes, and then walked back toward the tack room. He glanced in the direction of the house, and spotted Abigail's silhouette in an upstairs window.

The next morning Abigail came to him as he was feeding the chickens. "You heard the commotion last night? I don't know what they were doing, but you better go up there and check on our doe."

"Our doe?" Rafford said, knowing very well what she meant.

"Rafford, please don't – I really am worried. That deer and her fawn are in danger," her voice trembled with emotion.

"I know – I'll go up there later this morning. I promised Tyler that we would visit the doe today, anyway."

"Maybe Tyler should stay here," Abigail offered. "You don't know what you will find."

Rafford nodded, "You may be right, but either way, it could be a good lesson for him. But if you say no, I won't take him."

At that moment, the boy burst through the front door of the house and ran over to where they stood.

"Well, you're up and dressed early this morning," Abigail said cheerily.

"Rafford, we have to go check on the deer right away. Last night I heard gunshots and all kinds of noise, and it was coming from up there," the boy pointed toward Hart Mountain.

"I know - I heard it too," Rafford glanced at Abigail as he spoke. When she nodded he continued, "We'll go right after breakfast."

Rafford led Tyler along the timberline following the same path he had been using to check on the doe, nearly every day. The fresh dusting of snow on the trail would give them a good picture of whatever had happened last night, Rafford thought. When they reached the thicket where he usually found the doe, he showed Tyler where to sit and wait. Then he ventured slowly out into the open and crept toward the tree that sheltered the deer's nesting area. He moved slowly and deliberately, making as little noise as possible and pausing every few feet looking for movement. Finally, he reached out and touched the branches of the spruce tree. He knew the doe was not there, she would have been frightened into movement by now. Still he had to look.

He knelt down and peered under the tree; nothing. Rafford could see where the doe had been lying, but he could not tell when she had last been there. He did not touch anything, afraid that if she returned his scent would keep her away. He looked back at Tyler and shook his head no and motioned to the boy to wait. He looked around the tree for signs of the deer, but found no fresh tracks. There were no tracks of any kind – and no sign of snowmobiles. Whatever had gone on last night had not been here – it must have been farther up the trail perhaps where he had seen the ATVs before.

Rafford told Tyler what he had found then said, "Let's move on up the mountain a little farther and see if we can pick up her trail."

They walked for several minutes in silence. When they reached the clearing where Rafford had first spotted the ATVs, the snow was churned up with large clumps of earth leaving the soft ground scarred and broken. The smell of gasoline hung heavy in the damp morning air. Rafford knew that the snowmobiles had been right here last night and, as he expected, their trail led straight through a break in the fence line and on to gun club property. They looked closely but found no sign of the doe – nothing to say whether she was alive or dead.

"I don't know, Tyler" Rafford said. "The noise last night may have chased her deeper into the woods. If she is still around, she will probably go back to her nesting place. We'll have to be patient and watch for her."

"What if they shot her?" the boy asked.

"That's possible, but I don't see any sign of anything being shot here last night. They were making so much noise, they probably just scared her away," Rafford tried to sound convincing. "Let's walk along the fence line and make our way back toward her nesting place. Maybe we will find something."

They had not gone very far when Tyler spotted movement; something was thrashing around on the ground near the base of the fence. He pointed and whispered loudly, "Look! Over there – is it the deer?"

Rafford placed his hand firmly on the boy's shoulder, his mind racing. What if it was the doe and she was hurt? What would he do for the deer, and how would Tyler react?

"Stay behind me," he said as he moved forward toward the fence. He unsheathed his Buck knife and held his walking staff firmly in his other hand. Each new burst of movement was accompanied by a rustling sound in the brush. Although, he could not yet see what it was, Rafford was sure it was an animal, and from the sounds, it seemed to be struggling.

When they were about 10 feet away, Rafford stopped, "Well, it's not our deer," he whispered. "I can see brownish black fur, so it could be a small bear. Wait here, Tyler, while I get a closer look."

Rafford moved closer to the fence and then called out, "Tyler, come over here. It's a dog!"

The dog squirmed on the ground; his front legs were entangled in the barbed wire and were bleeding badly. He gave a low whimper that sounded like a weak attempt to growl. His fur was matted down with blood and dirt, especially on his right haunch. Rafford talked reassuringly to the frightened animal as he moved steadily closer. He reached slowly toward the dog's head, ignoring another growling whimper, and stroked him lightly behind the ears. From the dog's position, Rafford reasoned that he had been running away from something, or someone, when he slammed into the fence and was snagged by the steel barbs. That did not explain the blood on his haunches, but there would be time to figure that out once he was freed.   Rafford pulled a blue bandanna from his pocket, tied a loose knot in it and slipped the bandanna like a muzzle over the dog's snout.

"Just in case," he said to no one in particular.

Freeing the dog proved to be more difficult than he imagined. He worked to remove the barbs from the dog's legs, but each movement caused the animal to flinch and whimper. Each flinch, in turn, drove the barbs deeper into the swollen and bleeding flesh. Even with Tyler helping to hold the dog still, it took nearly thirty minutes for them to free him from the final barb.

Freed from the wire, the dog instinctively jumped to his feet, but then promptly fell back to the ground and lay still. Rafford removed the bandanna muzzle and wet it using the water bottle from his daypack. He gently daubed at the dog's wounds.

"Tyler, he is hurt pretty badly. We can't help him here, we have to get him back to the house and call the vet."

"He won't die, will he?" the boy sounded worried and scared.

"I don't know. I do know that his best chance is for us to get him to the vet. Can you help me?"

Tyler nodded seriously, "Yes. What do you want me to do?"

Rafford answered, but the roar of an approaching snowmobile drowned out his words. In only a few seconds, George Harder appeared astride a huge black snowmobile. He stopped directly across from them on the gun club side of the fence line.

"Well, what have we here -- a rescue mission?" Harder asked.

"Is this your doing, Harder?" Rafford said angrily. "What happened, you couldn't find any more wildlife to harass, so you turned on someone's lost dog?"

"I have no idea what you are talking about," Harder said with feigned innocence.

"We saw you last night," Tyler said angrily.

"And just who are you?" Harder glared at the boy. "Oh, wait, let me guess. You're the grandson, born of the woeful Carolyn. We need to talk, son. I can tell you some very interesting stories about your mother. You would be surprised."

"Harder," Rafford snapped, "you have nothing to say that either of us cares to listen to, except maybe explaining what happened to this dog."

"Oh, I see," Harder said with a leer, "I should have guessed. Abigail is a little old for you, isn't she? Now, Carolyn, on the other hand..."

Rafford glared at him, but did not say anything for a moment. When he spoke the anger in his voice was barely controlled, "So, just how fast does that machine go?"

Harder looked quizzically at him, and then answered "I've hit eighty miles an hour on a frozen lake but here, on these trails, I'm lucky to break thirty."

"Thirty miles an hour," Rafford mused, "Isn't that dangerous – I mean, what if there were a chain, say, strung across the trail? At that speed, it would be pretty tough to see something like that, wouldn't it?"

"That sounds like a threat to me," Harder barked.

"Take it any way you want, but if I were you, I'd be real careful the next time you go riding around on private property jacklighting deer - or dogs."

"You don't know what you are getting into, Brown. If anyone should be careful, it's you," Harder said with a sneer. "And as for you, young man, don't believe everything you hear."

Harder revved the engine loudly, popped the clutch and roared away, spraying snow and mud against the fence.

"Let's get this dog out of here," Rafford said.

Rafford took off his coat and using his walking staff and Tyler's walking staff, he fashioned a stretcher for the dog. The animal whimpered, but did not resist when they dragged him onto the litter.

"It's a long walk back and this stretcher is going to get heavy, so tell me if you need to rest. I don't want to drop him. OK?"

Tyler nodded his agreement, seriously. Rafford could see the boy was frightened.

"Don't worry about George Harder and his snowmobile. Right now, this pup is depending on us. Are you ready?"

The walk back was long and tiring, but Tyler never complained. When they reached the house, Abigail called the veterinarian and in less than thirty minutes, Dr. Branson had an intravenous line running in the dog's front leg, while she cleaned the wound in his haunch.

"You were right – this is a gunshot wound," she said with a mixture of surprise and anger. "The bullet passed through the soft flesh, right here," she pointed with her finger. "It could have been much worse - you are a lucky boy," she said as she scratched the dog on his exposed stomach.

"Gun club commandos," Rafford said under his breath.

"So, Maggie, do you know this dog?" Abigail asked.

"No – I've never seen him, before," the vet answered. "He's young and looks like he's been cared for – I assume he didn't have a collar or tags when you found him."

"Nothing," Rafford said.

"Can you take care of him for a few days, while he recovers, or do you want me to take him back to the clinic?"

Tyler, who had been sitting by the dog's head the whole time, quickly spoke up, "I can take care of him! Please, Grandma, let me take care of him."

"Well, he does seem to like you," Abigail said. "Maggie, what do we do about finding his owners?"

"I can help with that," the vet answered. "Sheriff Coleman and I have a regular procedure for dealing with strays. But, the truth is that we don't usually have much luck finding anyone, unless the dog has been reported missing by his owner. If no one claims him, would you want to keep him? Smokey might enjoy the company."

Tyler looked hopefully at his Grandmother. Abigail said, "We'll see. Right now, he needs someone to take care of him – and he needs a name. What shall we call him, Tyler?"

"I don't know," the boy answered, seriously. "I've never named anything, before."

Abigail smiled, "Well, you think on it. Since you're going to be the one to take care of him, you should be the one to give him a name. For now, we'll just call him, Dog."

⤌⤍

Chapter Twelve

R afford saw Amos Kreal walk in just as Dr. Branson was disinfecting the last of Dog's lacerations from the barbed wire. Tyler excitedly told him about what he had seen the night before and how he and Rafford went looking for the doe but found Dog, instead. He never mentioned George Harder.

Amos listened patiently to the boy's story then asked, "So, you never saw the doe, Tyler?"

Tyler slumped forward as if Amos' question had knocked the air out of him, "I was so worried about Dog, I..."

"It's OK, son, I'm sure she's hiding somewhere out there. She'll turn up just fine," he reassured him.

Amos followed Rafford through the barn to muck out an empty stall so Dog would have a place to recuperate.

"I hear you and Tyler had quite a morning."

"Yeah – frankly a bit more excitement than I wanted."

Amos pitched fresh hay into the stall while Rafford filled in the gaps in Tyler's narrative, including their confrontation with George Harder.

"I may have underestimated Harder, "Amos said. "I never had no trouble with him, but Larry over at the Agway, tells me he can be mean and nasty. I guess he's been throwing his weight around lately. He claims the new owners of the gun club have big plans and the money and political connections down in Albany to back them up. Shoot, I don't think Harder even knew Albany was the state capital before they came along. But Larry says we should be careful. You remember that snowshoer I told you about – the one that got run off the trail? Larry says that Harder went after him on purpose – said that the guy had complained to the DEC about gun club members jacklighting deer. "

"I can't say that I'm surprised," answered Rafford.

"Just don't let him get under your skin - he wants to provoke you."

"Why would he care about me?"

"He don't care about you! But he thinks he can use you, and the boy, to get to Abigail. Larry says that they have Rodney Paige, the Town Supervisor, finagling with the town's land use plan so that if Abigail wants to sell Deer Run, neighboring property owners would have right of first refusal. Deer Run only has one neighboring owner, besides the State of New York – the Black Stag Gun Club. She would have no choice; she'd have to sell Deer Run to them."

"So, she won't sell. She'll keep Deer Run," Rafford replied.

"Rafford, you may not have noticed, but Abigail and me, well we aren't getting any younger. Sooner or later, she's going to have to do something. Carolyn is her only family and I can't see her keeping the place up like her mother has done. So, if the land doesn't stay in the family, she'll have no choice but to sell," the old man's voice sounded worried.

"Well, for the time being, you and I will have to be sure that Harder remains disappointed. I won't let him get to her – or to Tyler." Rafford paused then asked, "What was Harder trying to say about Carolyn? He made it sound like there was some big dark secret about her."

Amos just kept pitching hay and was slow to respond. Finally, he said, "I suspect you should ask Abigail about that."

Rafford thought about what Amos had told him – and what he had not told him – for the rest of the afternoon. He did not know how to ask Abigail about Carolyn and was not sure he had the right to ask anything. She caught him off-guard when she raised the subject with him that evening, after Tyler had gone upstairs to bed.

"So just what did George Harder have to say about Carolyn?" she asked.

"George Harder? He, uh," Rafford stammered.

"Rafford, I know he said something to you and Ty about Carolyn - the boy told me. So, what exactly, did he say?"

"He said he knew some things about her that Tyler should know, and he called her 'woeful Carolyn'. I cut him off before he could say anything else."

"So, when were you going to ask me what he was talking about?"

"I'm not sure it's any of my business."

As though she never heard his reply, Abigail began "Carolyn went through a pretty tough time after her brother Richie died. She blamed herself for his death since the accident happened when he was going to pick her up at a friend's house. The whole time he was in the hospital she stayed in his room, whispering to him, crying, and praying for him to wake up. He never did.

When he died, she was devastated. She didn't leave her room for days at a time. When she finally went back to school, she was only going through the motions. We didn't understand how serious the problem was until one day she passed out in class. The school nurse figured it out; she was using drugs – pills and alcohol that one of her friends had stolen from her mother. The poor girl was in agony, but we were so deep in our own grief that we didn't see it."

Rafford stared at his feet, as he listened, "Abigail, you don't need to explain this to me. Its none of my –"

Abigail cut him off; "Rafford, in the past couple of weeks, I've come to depend on you and to think of you as..." she paused as though searching for the right word. "I want you to know. Would you please pour a glass of port for me? There's a bottle in that corner cupboard. Pour one for yourself, too, if you like."

They sipped their drinks in silence for a minute, before Abigail continued, "We tried everything, but nothing we did seemed to reach her. She was so distant – I will never forget the empty look in her eyes. A few weeks after the incident at school, Carolyn ran away. She disappeared; we had no idea where she had gone. For nearly three months, Roger and I were distraught. First, we had lost Richie, then it seemed like we had lost Carolyn, too. Finally, the State Police found her up in Potsdam. She had made up this whole new identity for herself and was living with some college kids. She told them she had followed a boyfriend from Colorado - fifteen years old, but she had everyone believing she was in college."

Abigail shook her head and took a deep breath, then let it out with a sigh.

"We brought her home after a tearful reunion. She didn't mean to be hurtful to us; she just didn't know how to live with the hurt in her heart. She continued to be a tortured soul through most of her high school years. She wouldn't go to classes, so we arranged for tutors to teach her at home. She never ran away again, but we let her go where and when she wanted, as long as she told us. We couldn't make things better, so we just did what we could to help her cope. But people talk, and soon everyone was talking about "woeful Carolyn". Oh, they would make it sound compassionate, like they were concerned for the poor girl who had lost her brother. But, truth was, they were just plain gossiping about the girl who dressed in black all the time and who didn't go to school like the "normal" kids. They made her out to be some pitiful, crazed loon."

"What finally brought her out of it?" Rafford asked.

Abigail smiled wistfully, "When she was seventeen, she worked all summer for a family that moved in down the road. They hired her to help take care of their little girl. The girl had been born with multiple birth defects – something to do with some medication the mother had taken before she got pregnant. Alicia – that was her name – was three years old. She couldn't walk or speak. All that summer Carolyn spent every day with her – feeding her, changing her, doing everything for her. At first, Carolyn was afraid of the child – she didn't even want to touch her. But, she forced herself to get over her discomfort because she felt such sympathy for her. Sometime during that summer, her pity turned into the kind of love that Carolyn had never felt for anyone or anything. When it did, something changed in Carolyn, too and slowly she came back to us. I still don't know exactly what happened, but that unfortunate little girl gave me back my daughter."

That night, Rafford could not sleep. His mind overflowed with images, some old and some new. He pictured Carolyn as a teenager, full of life and promise, looking like she did in the photographs hanging on the upstairs wall. Then he saw her smile fade and her image darken into the brooding runaway that Abigail described, long black coat blowing in the wind and her eyes, empty and vacant. Rafford knew that look intimately, not from Carolyn, but from another face. Her image gradually faded and was replaced by the face of Alicia, as Rafford imagined her, body misshapen but her spirit still bright and very much alive. Alicia's face slowly transformed into Tyler's; the boy smiling broadly as he had when he took the dogsled around the yard for the first time. Rafford felt the corners of his own mouth turn upward, responding to the boy's sheer joy. And then, Casey came to him, just as she did nearly every night, and Rafford's smile melted away. He was resigned, powerless to stop it; he knew the dream would come again tonight. He would follow her down the path and, once again, watch her vanish into the void beyond the wall.

A distant voice deep in his thoughts spoke to him, "Carolyn, Alicia, Tyler, Casey. Promises kept, promises broken, promises never to be."

What?

Promises?

Rafford strained to hear the voice more clearly, as he drifted deeper and deeper into sleep. The dream was irresistible; he followed Casey down the path.

Rafford was up early the next morning, tired from a restless night. He headed straight to the barn to check on Dog. As soon as he opened the stall door, Dog was on his feet, tail wagging but whimpering softly. He limped across the stall and rubbed against Rafford's leg.

"You look a lot better this morning," Rafford said, scratching Dog behind the ears. He checked the dressing Dr. Branson had applied to the bullet wound on the dog's haunch and then, satisfied with Dog's condition, he left the barn and headed for the livestock pen.

The morning chores were routine for him now, although the antics of the three goats frequently surprised him. When he had milked the goats, fed, and watered the livestock, he went back to the tack room and quickly packed a few essentials in his daypack. He knew Abigail would be making breakfast about then, but he did not have time this morning. Instead, he shouldered his daypack and set off at a brisk pace toward Hart Mountain.

He was relieved to find that the doe had returned to her nesting spot under the spruce tree. Wherever she had gone yesterday, she had remained safe. She stood nibbling on one of the alder branches that he had left for her earlier in the week. Her belly was so swollen that she could barely walk. The fawn will come soon, Rafford thought, still not sure what he would do when she gave birth. For the moment, he would be content to check on her daily, but always from a safe distance. He was sure at times that the doe sensed his presence. She would gaze in his direction, standing still as a statue for minutes on end. Watching through his binoculars, Rafford could see her nostrils flare as she tried to pick up his scent. If she knew he was there, she showed no fear.

When Rafford returned to Deer Run, he saw Sheriff Coleman's squad car parked by the house. Rafford dropped his daypack in the tack room, and then went to find Abigail and the Sheriff. As he expected, they were in the kitchen where the Sheriff was enjoying a slice of Abigail's apple pie.

"Morning, Sheriff," Rafford offered when Coleman mumbled something to him through a mouthful of pie. "So, did Dr. Branson tell you about the dog? He's doing much better, today. Have you seen him?"

The Sheriff nodded, "Tyler took me to the barn. Nice dog – lucky you two found him when you did. We'll try to find his owner, but most times these strays are never claimed."

Abigail interjected, "Don't go looking too hard, Curtis. There are those around here that would be glad to have Dog stay with us, permanently."

"If he stays here," Rafford said, "we'll have to keep him away from that gun club bunch. Can't you do something about them, Sheriff? They're bad news, especially, George Harder."

"Watch what you say, Rafford," Coleman answered. "You're already on thin ice."

"Thin ice? What are you talking about?" Rafford asked.

"George Harder filed a formal complaint, yesterday; he said you threatened him."

"What!"

"He said you threatened to," Coleman pulled a paper from his pocket and read aloud, "string chains across public snowmobile trails in order to cause bodily harm to him and other members of Black Stag Gun Club."

"He filed a complaint against me? He's the one jacklighting deer, trespassing on private land, and shooting dogs – but he filed a complaint against me!"

Abigail spoke before Coleman could respond, "Calm down, Rafford. Curtis knows what's going on here. He's just doing his job."

Sheriff Coleman nodded, "This is a formal complaint, so I am required to interview you and the boy."

"No – you leave Tyler out of this!" Rafford said firmly.

"Too late – I already talked to him," Coleman answered. "He told me what happened. I believe him – and you. But you better cool off, because right now, if anything did happen to Harder or the others, you could be in a whole boatload of trouble."

Abigail reassuringly placed her hand on Rafford's shoulder. "It's going to be alright. Curtis will file his report and that will be the end of it."

Rafford shook his head, "No, it won't be the end of it. Harder isn't going to go away. Whatever he's up to, he isn't going to stop. Amos says he's trying to provoke me to get at you. I won't let that happen, Abigail. That's no threat Sheriff; it's just the plain truth."

Abigail nodded, "I know George Harder. This has been going on for years – even when he worked for the town, before he was hired to run the gun club. They started on Roger, but they couldn't push him around. So once he was out of the way, they decided to push me. Well, I don't push either. Harder and his cronies won't be satisfied until they have the full run of this entire valley, and I am not going to let that happen."

The finality in Abigail's tone ended the conversation. The three of them sat in silence for a few moments, and then Rafford got up, nodded at the sheriff and headed back to the barn.

When he was gone, Sheriff Coleman turned to Abigail, "I know you don't want to hear this, but I still feel uneasy about him. My sources haven't turned up anything, yet, but I'm going to keep looking."

"Curtis, will you please leave it alone! Rafford told you what happened with Harder, and Tyler said the same thing. Granted, we don't know much about his past, but he has never done anything to make me worry."

"But what if Harder is telling the truth? Rafford does seem to have a temper – and, well, who knows what might set him off," Coleman answered.

"George Harder is enough to set me off!" Abigail said impatiently. "If you find out anything about Rafford that seems to be a problem, I will deal with it. Until then, Rafford Brown is welcome here, which is more than I can say for you, unless you back off!"

Rafford found Tyler sitting on the floor in Dog's stall. Dog was stretched out on his side, his head resting in Tyler's lap. Behind him, Rafford heard a low growl. He turned to find that Smokey had followed him from the house and the old dog was not pleased about this interloper. Either Dog did not hear him, or he did not care, because he showed no reaction.

Tyler looked up and Rafford said, "I guess Smokey is jealous. How is our patient doing?"

"He's good, I guess," the boy answered. "Sheriff Coleman is here; he asked me a lot of questions."

Rafford nodded, "I just finished talking to him in the house. Don't worry about him, or George Harder. Everything will be OK. You know, I bet Smokey is hoping you will run him in the sled today."

"I will. Uncle Amos is coming over after lunch to teach me some more."

"Uncle Amos?" Rafford said with a smile.

"Yeah; I know he's not really my uncle, but Grandma said I had to call him Mr. Kreal, and he didn't like that. So, he said to call him 'Uncle Amos'. Is that OK?" Tyler asked.

"That is up to your Grandmother, but when your 'uncle' gets here, you should ask him about training Dog to run the sled with Smokey. He looks like he would make a good sled dog," Rafford smiled at the boy. "Well, I've got firewood to split," he said as he headed for the door.

That afternoon, Amos had Tyler and Smokey running the sled around the barn. Dog watched them through the open barn door, barking and yipping each time they came into view. Suddenly, Dog rose up and put his front paws on top of the stall door and with one powerful thrust of his hind legs, he scrambled over the door and charged out of the barn. Dog chased after Tyler and Smokey, caught up with them, and began trotting along next to Smokey, matching him stride for stride. They continued side by side until Tyler stopped the sled by the open barn door.

Amos laughed, "Well, how about that? It looks like Dog knows something about sledding! Did you see, Tyler, how he matched his pace to Smokey? It looked like he was in harness with him. Once he is a little stronger, we'll have to give him a chance to pull. For now, take the sled once more around the barn and let Dog run alongside."

❧ ❧

Chapter Thirteen

R afford finally ran out of excuses to avoid going to church with Abigail. For weeks he had talked his way around Abigail's invitations, but he knew she would not stop asking. Sunday morning, after breakfast, the three of them loaded into Abigail's truck and headed down Route 30 to Cold River Community Church.

Rafford wanted to sit in the back pew, but Abigail insisted they would sit together where her family always sat – two rows from the front on the right side of the small sanctuary. He noticed Abigail smiling and nodding at the others in the congregation as he and Tyler followed her down the aisle and took their seats.

Rafford had not been in church for a long time, but little had changed. The hymns, the prayers, the Bible readings all had a familiar feel to him. When Pastor Joanne invited the children to come forward Tyler reluctantly joined three little girls and a toddler boy still in diapers. The children sat around the Pastor on the steps that led up to the altar while she told them a story about Jesus. Rafford heard little of what she said; his attention was riveted on the little girl sitting next to Tyler. She looked so much like his daughter Casey that it took his breath away. Her eyes, the way her pigtails swayed when she walked and the sound of her laughter – it was as if Casey had come back to him. Rafford found himself gasping for air as though he was suffocating. When the children came back to their seats, Rafford stood up to let Tyler into the pew and then, instead of sitting down he walked back up the aisle and out the front door of the church. Abigail watched him go, but did not follow.

Rafford sat on the front steps of the church and listened, halfheartedly, to the rest of the service. When the front doors opened and people began to file out, he stood to the side watching for Abigail and Tyler.

Abigail never asked Rafford why he left, but once they were in the truck she said, "Pastor Joanne asked me to tell you that she hoped you might come to church again. She's really a good person, Rafford; I think you might like her."

Rafford nodded his head but said nothing.

"Anyway," Abigail continued, "I invited her to stop by this week for coffee, so you will have another chance to get acquainted."

Three days later, Rafford came out of the barn with a wheelbarrow load of soiled straw for the compost pit and found Pastor Joanne walking toward him from the house.

"Good morning, Reverend."

"Good morning! There's always work to be done, isn't there?"

"I think Abigail is in the kitchen..." Rafford offered.

"She is, but actually I was hoping to talk with you for a few minutes. Is that OK with you?"

"Sure, I suppose this is as good a time as any to take a break," Rafford replied.

They stood by the livestock pen and made small talk for a while, and then Pastor Joanne said, "It was good to have you join us in church on Sunday. I hope you will come back again."

"I'm sorry about leaving early –"

"No apology or explanation needed. I always come into church thinking that whoever is there is supposed to be there. If someone is missing or leaves early I don't take it personally. The Bible says, 'For everything there is a season...' When the time is right – God's time, that is – then we will see what happens," she answered.

"God and I haven't exactly been on good terms, lately. Maybe it's just not my 'season' yet," Rafford said.

"I don't know why that is. If you want to talk about it, I would be happy to listen. But either way, I hope you know that God is a god of grace. There isn't anything we can do that God will not forgive."

Rafford winced slightly, "Well, you see, the problem is not God forgiving me – it's me forgiving God. Forgiveness may be God's strong suit, but it is not mine."

Pastor Joanne nodded knowingly.   "You may be surprised to learn you are not alone in that regard. Just about everyone I know has a hard time learning to forgive – even yours truly. I think Jesus understood that, too. When he taught his disciples how to pray he included the line, 'forgive us our trespasses as we forgive those who trespass against us'. I think his point was that forgiveness is a two-way street. Our own failings will be forgiven in the same way that we learn to forgive others."

"So, you mean God won't forgive me unless I forgive God?" Rafford asked.

"No! No, that's the good news of the Gospel. God's grace is a gift, one we don't have to earn and one we could never earn even if we tried. Jesus was talking about us forgiving one another but letting God's example of forgiveness teach us," she paused for moment and then continued. "Just what did God do that you cannot forgive, if you don't mind me asking?"

"You can ask but I don't know you well enough yet to answer. But let me ask you something: If God is good, why is there so much evil and suffering in the world? I mean, if God created it all and saw that it was good, then how did the world get so messed-up?"

"You don't ask easy questions, do you?" she asked. "Theodicy – it's called theodicy – the existence of evil in a world created and ruled over by a good God. It's one of the classic questions theologians have argued over for centuries. The problem is that the only answers they can offer are philosophical answers which frankly are not much help for people like us wrestling with life's pains and problems. Their answers may stimulate our theoretical thinking about God, but they do little to build up our faith and they do even less to help us cope with the difficulties of life that can be overwhelming."

"Meaning no disrespect," Rafford said, "but that sounds like you don't have an answer, either."

The Pastor replied, "Oh, I have an answer, one that works for me, but I can't promise it will work for you. Especially since I don't know what it is that you blame on God."

"Now you've got me curious," Rafford said. "What is your answer?"

"Well, first of all, I think there is a difference between suffering and evil. I think that evil is intentional; it is a choice that someone makes to be hurtful or harmful. It comes from our free will. God gives us the ability to choose help or harm, love or hate, good or evil. Being imperfect human beings who don't always make the best choices, sometimes evil wins out. God created us to live with and live for one another, to live in love. But since love must always be freely given, God had to give us the ability to choose not to love. Loving cannot be required, we must always have the option of choosing not to love. When we choose not to love bad things happen and we have no one to blame but ourselves. It is not God's fault, it's our own doing."

Rafford nodded slowly then said, "So God did not create evil but God left the door open for us to invite evil in."

"I haven't thought of it that way before but I like that analogy. But what matters is not whether it works for me, but whether it works for you. In the end, each of us needs to come to grips with these things for ourselves if we want to find God."

"So that's it?" Rafford said.

"No, that's just the first part. The second part goes something like this. It seems to me that pain and suffering are facts of life in this world. Stuff happens – tragedies, accidents, illnesses even death. God did not create this world or life in this world to be eternal goodness – that is what we have to look forward to in the next life. The theologians would say, you can't have sweet without sour, light without dark, happiness without suffering. What is darkness? They would say it is the absence of light. So suffering is the absence of goodness, it is the other side of the coin."

Rafford interjected, "OK, but where is this good-God when God's people are in pain, suffering even dying? How can a good God tolerate that?"

She answered, "I read once of a theologian whose son was killed as a young man in an auto accident. Someone asked him how he could still love God when God had taken his son away from him. The father was furious. He answered God had not taken his son. It was not God's doing that his son was driving too fast on a rainy night or that he had probably had too much to drink. When his son died on that lonely stretch of highway he was sure that God was there with him, the first to weep over the tragic loss of a young man's life.

Rafford, I believe God is always with us, as near as our own breath. When we celebrate God rejoices with us. When we mourn God shares our grief. And when we are in pain, suffering under the hurts of this world, God knows our agony. God knows it because it because Jesus lived it. Through Jesus, God lived our life and God died our death and in Jesus' suffering on the cross God came to know the darkest side of human existence. In that moment, God resolved never to leave us alone in this life, but to send God's Holy Spirit to be present with us, in us, always."

The two stood silently, watching three goats playfully knocking heads in the livestock pen.

Rafford broke the silence, "Thanks for that. I need to think about what you said for a while, but I appreciate your perspective. Maybe we can talk about it again, sometime?"

"Any time you would like," Pastor Joanne answered. "But you know, you can talk to God about it anytime. You may not have forgiven God for whatever you believe God did wrong, but God is still here with you. The God I know is both patient and persistent. When you are ready God will be right there."

Chapter Fourteen

Tyler and Dog were inseparable; as Dog grew stronger each day he followed Tyler everywhere he went. Abigail insisted that Dog sleep in the barn, at first, but Tyler begged and pleaded until she gave-in and let Dog sleep in the boy's room. She saw that it was senseless to argue; the two of them belonged together.

By the time Dr. Branson had removed the stitches from Dog's hind leg, Amos had made a two-dog harness for the sled. Dog took to the harness right away, as though he had pulled sleds before. At first Smokey growled and snarled, but Dog ignored his complaints. Once the two of them were pulling side-by-side, Smokey settled down and the two dogs teamed well together. Dog was younger, stronger and faster than Smokey but, instinctively, he seemed to let the older dog set the pace, trotting alongside with his eyes straight ahead and his tail held high.

Amos set up a practice course for Tyler and they all watched the boy's confidence grow with each turn around the track. The course circled the barn, cut back between the livestock pen and the shed, turned down toward the riverbank, and then crossed back through the woods to finish in front of the barn. The course was not long, but working the turns and the path through the trees gave both the dogs and Tyler good practice.

"The boy has a soft hand," Amos said to Abigail as they stood on the porch watching Tyler skillfully turn the sled toward the river. "You know, for a city boy, he seems right at home here."

Abigail kept her eyes on the sled and smiled, "Watching him over the past couple of weeks has been very special. Sometimes he reminds me of Richie, at that age; but other times I look at him and I see Roger – the same curiosity, the same sense of wonder. Until now, Tyler never really spent much time here, but he acts like he feels that special bond to the Adirondacks that Roger had, as though he was born from this land. I can't help but wonder, what will happen when Carolyn comes back. I'm afraid he's got this place in his blood, now, and the thought of moving away is not going to sit well with him."

As he pulled the sled to a stop by the barn, Tyler called out, "Uncle Amos!"

Abigail turned quickly and gave Amos a piercing look, "Uncle Amos? Where in the world did that come from?"

Amos pretended not to hear, but instead hopped down the porch steps two at a time as he headed toward the boy. Abigail followed close behind.

"Uncle Amos, this course is too easy. Can I take the sled up toward Hart Mountain? Maybe I can find the doe."

Abigail answered before Amos could, "Not yet, Tyler. You need to keep practicing and the dogs need to work up to something that difficult. For now, you stay close to home and, remember, I don't want you to use the sled unless 'Uncle' Amos is here with you."

Tyler began to argue, but Abigail held firm. The boy was still complaining about Abigail's rules as he and Amos were putting the sled away.

Amos cut him off in mid-sentence, "Stop right there, boy. Your grandmother is probably the finest woman in these mountains, and I won't tolerate anybody talking her down. You are one lucky boy to have a grandmother that loves you and cares about what happens to you. So, if she says no about something, you just say, 'Yes, Grandma' and do what she tells you."

Amos saw the dejected look on Tyler's face. "I won't be here the next couple of days – I've got to go over to Burlington to check on my sister. But when I get back on Saturday, let's see what we can do about a new practice run."

The rest of that day, and all day Thursday, Tyler was wound up tighter than a coiled spring. Abigail tried to keep him busy, but all he would talk about was sledding. Every time he went near the barn, the two dogs excitedly followed. Dog ran circles around him, jumping and yipping; even Smokey seemed more lively. Abigail wondered whether Tyler or the two dogs were more disappointed that the sled remained covered in the barn.

Late Thursday afternoon, when Abigail went to visit a neighbor and Rafford was inside the house cleaning the wood stove, Tyler slipped out of the house and quickly walked to the barn with the two dogs happily in tow. He quietly pushed the sled out the back door toward the woods. He had never harnessed the dogs by himself, but he had watched Amos do it many times. Smokey stood quietly while Tyler slipped on the rope harness and fastened the metal clips. Dog, however, was a bundle of energy, and it took several tries, before Tyler finally got the harness on him. He checked everything, twice, to be sure it looked exactly like when Amos did it. Then he pulled on his gloves, pushed the sled gently and gave the dogs a quiet, 'Hup'.

At the exact moment that he gave the command to pull, a rabbit popped out of the woodpile, right in front of the dogs. The rabbit froze in place, for just a moment, trembling almost imperceptibly. Dog, too, trembled for a moment, then he wailed a sound Tyler had never heard before; a sound somewhere between a long howl and a bark. The chase was on. The rabbit darted away toward the woods and Dog exploded after him, driving hard with all four paws. Smokey, startled by Dog's bark, spotted the rabbit and joined in the chase. The sled shot forward so quickly that it nearly pulled Tyler off his feet. In a blur, they rocketed down the trail with both dogs digging deep into the snow, and Tyler scrambling to stay on his feet. He ran as fast as he could, shouting at the dogs to stop, but they did not respond. He jumped on the sled runners but he was not heavy enough to slow them down. He tried dragging his boots in the snow, but to no avail; the sled kept picking up speed, going faster and faster.

They flew through the woods, weaving between trees, under low branches and bouncing through the deep snow. The dogs were running full speed when Tyler realized that they were headed for the river. He took a firm grip on the crossbar, determined to stop the sled before they reached the ice-covered river. When the sled broke through the tree line into a clearing, he saw his chance and jammed his boots deep into the snow. The sled skidded to the left and, at the same moment, the rabbit veered hard to the right followed by the dogs, in close pursuit. The sled skidded sideways and slammed into a tree stump barely hidden under the snow. Before Tyler knew what happened, the sled popped up into the air and then flipped over onto its side throwing him hard to the ground. He tumbled over and over, down the hill finally coming to rest on a patch of ice that covered a small pond. The ice was not thick enough to hold Tyler's weight, and before he realized where he was, the ice gave way, and dropped him into the frigid water. The pond was shallow at this spot, so Tyler quickly scrambled to his feet, and sloshed his way out of the pond. His clothes were soaked through from the waist down, and he was so cold he could hardly breathe. He scrambled back up the hill, and found the sled lying on one side with the two dogs still in harness and panting hard.

He wrestled the sled back to an upright position and heard a sickening crack as it settled back on the runners. The left side runner had broken away from the sled, and the pieces dangled loosely. He sat down in the snow, and stared at the broken sled. He tried to fit the pieces back together, but his hands would not stop shaking. His teeth were chattering, too, and soon his entire body was shivering uncontrollably. He unhooked the dog harness from the sled and started trudging through the snow back toward the house.

As he neared the barn, the two dogs ran ahead of him, barking and wagging their tails. Tyler looked up, and saw Rafford coming toward him.

"What happened to you?" Rafford asked as he came closer.

Tyler tried to answer but he could not speak.

"Tyler, you're shaking!" Rafford said as he put his arms around the boy and pulled him close. The boy could not stop shivering so he threw him over one shoulder and hurried back toward the tack room.

Rafford stoked the fire in the wood stove, and the warmth of the fire quickly filled the room. He helped Tyler out of his cold wet clothes and then wrapped him in two woolen blankets. He took his old Sierra cup outside and returned with it full of snow. He poured hot coffee from the pot on the wood stove over the snow, testing the temperature with his finger until it was cool enough to drink. He stirred in two heaping spoons of sugar and gave it to Tyler.

"Just sip it slowly, Tyler."

While Tyler drank the coffee, Rafford removed the rest of the sled harness from Dog and Smokey. The two dogs curled-up, side-by-side, on the floor near the warm stove.

When Tyler had warmed up enough to talk, he told Rafford what had happened. He never looked at Rafford, instead he stared down at the floor through the entire story.

Rafford listened in silence. When Tyler stopped talking, Rafford stood up, picked up the rope harness and walked to the door.

"You stay here and finish getting warm. I'm going to drag the sled back here before it gets dark. Smokey, Dog! Let's go!" Rafford took the dogs and left.

Tyler sat for a while sipping the coffee and feeling miserable about what he done. He stood up and a sharp pain shot through his right leg, all the way from his back down to his foot. He limped around the room, twisting and stretching, trying to make the pain go away. He felt a knot at the base of his spine that made him wince each time he touched it.

He had never been in Rafford's room before. He looked around but there was not much to see. The woodstove and Rafford's bunk filled most of the room, leaving very little space to move about. A worn backpack hung on the wall next to a small shelf. The shelf held a comb, razor, toothbrush and a Bible sitting atop a small leather-covered notebook. Tyler looked around nervously, and then picked up the notebook. The leather cover was buttery soft from years of handling, and it had the monogram RWB in the lower right corner. He opened the notebook and fanned through page after page of journal entries and rough pencil sketches, mostly landscapes of places Rafford had stayed. Tucked between pages in the front of the Bible, he found a photograph of a little girl with blond pigtails and a happy smile that showed one tooth missing.

Just then Dog came bursting through the door with Smokey right behind. Tyler quickly returned the Bible and notebook to the shelf, but he did not notice when the photograph fell out and fluttered to the floor. When Rafford walked in, Tyler was crouched down scratching Dog behind the ears.

"Feeling better?" Rafford asked.

Tyler nodded, "My back and leg hurt, but I'll be OK. I guess I'm better than the sled, at least nothing is broken."

"You're worried about the sled?" Rafford mused. "It's not that bad."

Tyler looked surprised, "But I saw the pieces – it was broken in two!"

Rafford smiled, "All you did was finish the job your Grandfather started."

"On Suicide Hill?" Tyler interrupted.

Rafford laughed, "Yup, the runner broke free from the frame right where he had cracked it years ago. We can fix it."

Rafford took off his coat and hung it on a nail next to his backpack. He bent over to brush the snow off his pants and spotted the picture lying on the floor. He picked it up and looked directly at Tyler.

"Were you going through my things?" his voice was soft, but firm.

"I was looking around – I didn't mean to –" Tyler stammered. "Yes, sir; I'm sorry."

"I don't have many secrets, Tyler, but I do expect you to respect my privacy. Do you understand?"

The boy nodded, keeping his eyes down.

Rafford sat down on the bunk, next to Tyler, and held the photograph so they both could see it.

"Casey, that's her name. She is – was - my daughter."

Tyler looked up at him, "I didn't know you had a family."

"I don't, anymore," Rafford gazed at the photograph as if it might disappear if he looked away.

"Casey always made me feel special. I could not believe that this perfect little girl was my daughter. It's hard to explain, but being Casey's father meant more to me than anything. If I could have her back, I would..." his voice trailed off, choked with emotion.

"She looks happy in the picture," Tyler said tentatively.

Rafford nodded, "That's the way she was – always smiling, full of life. Even though I miss her terribly, every time I look at her picture she makes me smile."

"Why did you say she *was* your daughter? Where did she go?"

"Casey," Rafford took a deep breath before continuing, and when he spoke again, his voice was barely a whisper. "Casey died, not long after this picture was taken. She was only four years old. It was October and our neighbors had covered their swimming pool for the winter. Rainwater would collect on top of the pool cover and birds would come to splash around in the puddles. Casey loved to stand by the fence and watch them. But on this one particular day, she must have squeezed through the fence, probably just to get a better look at the birds. Somehow, she fell into the pool. The water was not very deep, but her legs became entangled in the pool cover and she drowned.

My wife found her. I wasn't home when it happened, so I couldn't..." Rafford paused, and then whispered with powerful conviction, "I should have been there. She needed her Daddy to keep her safe. I should have been there."

Tyler did not know what to do. He watched the tears form in Rafford's eyes and trickle slowly down his cheeks. He felt like he should say something, but he could not; he wanted to cry, too.

The sound of a car coming up the driveway broke the silence. Abigail was home.

Rafford wiped his sleeve across his face and said, "Your clothes are still damp, but you probably should put them on and get back to the house. You can change into dry things before dinner."

Tyler dressed and as he left the tack room, Rafford stopped him and said, "You're a good boy, Tyler. Don't be too hard on yourself. Things happen, sleds get broken, it's not the end of the world. The things that really matter, things like your family, the people who love you, they won't change just because you make a mistake or do something wrong. You may not believe me, but all the broken dogsleds in the world couldn't make your Grandmother love you any less."

At dinner that night, Rafford noticed that Tyler seemed more at ease with him, as if they had been friends for a long, long time. He noticed Abigail watching them and wondered if she could see the change, too.

"So, what did you two do this afternoon while I was visiting Mable Burch?" she asked.

Rafford answered quickly, "Not much; I cleaned out the woodstove and Tyler took the dogs out for some exercise. Nothing special."

"Is that all you did, Tyler?"

The boy stammered, "Uh, I guess so."

Tyler seemed relieved when Abigail changed the subject, "I was thinking, on the way home this afternoon, that it's time to go cut down that Christmas tree. Would you boys be able to do that, tomorrow?"

"Sure," Rafford said. "We can pack a lunch, cut down the tree and maybe even check on the doe."

Abigail went on, "If you'd like, you could even drive the dogsled up there, instead of the pickup, to bring the tree back. Would you like that, Tyler?"

Tyler kept his eyes downcast, "Grandma, the dogsled..."

Rafford cut him off, "It's okay Tyler, I'll have the sled finished in time. I promised Tyler that I would tighten the sled runners – one of them seemed pretty loose the last time he had the sled out. I'll get it done right after morning chores, and then we can go after the tree. Okay?"

Tyler nodded at him, "Sure. I'll get up early and help you with the goats."

Carolyn called after dinner, as she had nearly every night since going to Texas. However, this call did not follow the usual pattern. Instead of going on excitedly about dog sledding, the doe and his other daily adventures, Tyler asked his mother about her trip.

"Mom, did you find a job there?"

"No, not yet Ty, but I have two more interviews next week, before I come back to New York," Carolyn replied.

"Mom, can't you just come home, now?" the boy asked tentatively.

"Why, Tyler? Is something wrong?"

"No, nothing's wrong. It's just..." he took a long pause and then said very quickly, "I don't want to go to Texas; I just want you to come home."

"Tyler, I don't want to talk about this now. I know you don't want to leave your friends in Boston, but this move is important for us and for my career."

"But, Mom!" Tyler started.

"Not now, Tyler!" Carolyn's voice filled with frustration. "I will be back next week and we can talk about it then. Now, let me talk to your Grandma."

"What's wrong with Tyler?" Carolyn asked when Abigail took the phone.

"Nothing is wrong. He's fine, I think he is just confused about where you two are going to call home. Once you get back, I'm sure everything will sort itself out," Abigail said the words and tried to sound like she believed them. "Don't worry; we'll see you next week."

✌✪✪

Chapter Fifteen

R afford was up before dawn working to reattach the sled runner, and he was still working on it when Tyler finished the morning chores. The boy came into the barn and stood watching him work.

"Can I do anything to help?" he asked.

"I'm just about finished. Come over here and see what I did. You never know, you may have to fix it yourself, the next time."

Rafford showed Tyler the pieces of wood that he had cut to bracket the break in the runner. "We probably should have Amos help us make a new runner, but for now, this brace will be strong enough. It doesn't look as nice as the original, but it will work."

Tyler helped Rafford sand the rough edges of the brace, and then brush on a protective coating of spar varnish. It was too cold in the barn for the varnish, so they dragged the sled into the tack room to dry.

They were ready to go by late morning. Tyler waved to Abigail, who watched from the porch, then he gave a quiet "Hup" to the dogs and they set off at a slow trot. Rafford walked close behind the sled, his walking staff in hand and his snowshoes strapped to his daypack, just in case. The dogs wanted to run, but Tyler kept them in check, maintaining a steady, comfortable pace toward Hart Mountain.

They walked for nearly forty-five minutes before they reached the Christmas tree that they had picked out with Abigail. Their strips of red and blue cloth stood out amid the snow-frosted branches of the tree.

"It looks like it's already decorated," Tyler said, laughing. "All we need is the angel on the top."

"You're right," Rafford answered. "It's almost too pretty to cut down. Let's have lunch first; we can admire the tree while we eat."

Abigail had packed a lunch sack with ham and cheese sandwiches on thick slices of her homemade honey wheat bread, apples and two enormous oatmeal raisin cookies.

"Your Grandma is about the best cook I have ever known," Rafford said while wiping crumbs from his face.

Tyler nodded agreement, then, after a moment, he said, "Why didn't you tell her what really happened with the dogsled?"

"Why didn't you?" Rafford replied.

"I wanted to, but, you said you would fix it and..."

"And that was better than telling her that you disobeyed her," Rafford finished the boy's sentence. "Tyler, I said what I did so that you would have a way out. But it was your choice – it is always your choice – whether to take that way out or not. Abigail has been very good to me, and I wouldn't do anything to hurt her, but she is your Grandmother, and that means a lot more. So you have to decide for yourself what you should do."

"My mother always says to tell the truth," Tyler said. "She says she will never be angry with me, if I just tell her the truth. But if I lie to her..." he left the consequences unsaid.

"Truthfulness is a good thing. Maybe, you should tell your Grandmother what really happened. What do you think?"

"I don't know; I'm just a kid. You're an adult - what do think I should do?"

"You don't think adults always know the answers, do you? We surely don't always do the right thing! If something is important to you, then you need to make that decision yourself."

Tyler began to protest, "But I don't –"

Rafford interrupted, "Trust yourself, Tyler; just trust yourself. You may be young, but you know what is important. I hate to tell you this, but for the rest of your entire life you are going to have tough decisions to make, and most of the time you probably won't be sure about what you should do. So, this is good practice. Trust yourself; get to know what matters to you, and then make your choice. If you trust yourself, you will always find the right answer."

"Pastor Joanne, in church, said we should trust Jesus. She said if we don't know the right thing to do, Jesus will help us decide."

"Pastor Joanne is a smart woman and I think she is right about Jesus. So you could say a prayer and ask Jesus to help you figure things out, but sometimes just thinking about things, about what is right and wrong will work too. If you listen closely while you are thinking, sometimes you can hear a little voice inside telling you what to do. Some people call that voice your conscience, some people call that voice Jesus or God's Holy Spirit. But remember, Jesus can help you know what to do, but you still need to be the one to do it."

Rafford broke off a piece of bread from his sandwich and flipped it casually toward a nearby fir tree. In a moment, a brilliant red cardinal dropped out of the tree, scooped up the bread and disappeared back into the branches.

"Well, as pretty as that tree looks out here in the woods, I bet it will look even better in your Grandmother's front room. Are you ready to cut it down?"

Tyler brought the folding saw from the sled. Rafford put the saw together and handed it back to Tyler.

"You want me to cut it down?" Tyler said incredulously.

"Sure, it's time you learned," Rafford answered. "Crawl under there and work slowly until you get the feeling of the saw. Try to cut the tree as close to the ground as you can."

Tyler worked the saw carefully, stopping several times to check on his progress. Finally, the tree gave way and Rafford gently pulled it toward him and laid it on the ground. A few minutes later, the tree safely rested on the dog sled tied securely to the side rails. They harnessed the dogs and prepared to leave.

"Do you remember the way we went last time, when we spotted the doe?" Rafford asked.

Tyler pointed, "We went toward that rocky point. Do you think she's had her fawn, yet?" Tyler asked.

"Her fawn? I didn't know you knew about that," Rafford answered.

"Uncle Amos told me, and he also told me that the fawn might not live through the winter, unless we help," the boy said, matter-of-factly.

Rafford was relieved, "Tyler, are you sure you're only ten? Sometimes you seem a lot older to me. Okay, let's see if we can pick up her trail."

After they had walked for only a few minutes, Tyler called to the dogs to stop. "I see tracks in the snow, up ahead."

Rafford went ahead to check, and then came back to where Tyler waited.

"Are they deer tracks?" the boy asked.

"Not unless she is wearing hiking boots. I saw one set of boot prints and some dog tracks coming from the State Forest over there. They are fresh tracks, too, so whoever made them is probably nearby."

"Do you think it's someone from the gun club?"

"I doubt it; those guys never walk when they can ride. It's probably just a hiker or backpacker."

Just then, they heard a rustling movement in the brush behind them and a man walked toward them, followed by a beautiful silver and gray Malamute.

"Could be a hiker, or a backpacker; it might even be a park ranger," the man said as he came closer. "I hope you have a license to drive that dogsled, young man. And you, Rafford Brown, should know that you can't cut down trees in the people's forest."

Tyler looked fearfully at the Ranger and then at Rafford.

Rafford laughed, "Well, well, well, Travis Warner! What are you doing here?"

"You know me, Rafford; I'm always on the lookout for tree-poaching, dog-sled driving, desperados!" Warner answered. "So, who's your partner driving the get-a-way sled?"

"Travis, this is Tyler Morgan; his grandmother is Abigail Sherwood. She owns –"

"Deer Run," Warner broke in. "I've heard about her – all the Rangers have."

Rafford said to Tyler, "Tyler, this is Travis Warner, the hardest working Ranger in the Adirondacks." Turning back to Warner, he nodded toward the dog and said, "Who is your four legged friend?"

"This is Storm – isn't he a handsome devil?" Warner laughed. "His dog-sledding genes must be heating up, just looking at that sled of yours, Tyler."

Rafford bent down and scratched Storm behind the ears, "So, Travis, what are you doing here? You weren't reassigned to this district, were you? I mean, I know you love the St. Regis area."

Warner shook his head, "No – that is still my district. Actually, I'm here as a favor to an old friend. Curtis Coleman called me a few days ago, asking about you. We got to talking, and he told me about your run-ins with the Black Stag gunners. Well, I had a few days off, so I decided to come take a look."

"I didn't realize that Curtis Coleman was an old friend of yours," Rafford said somberly.

"He isn't," Warner said with a smile as he reached out and put his hand on Rafford's shoulder. "So, where are you boys headed?"

"You won't believe this, but Tyler and I are on our way to check up on a doe, a pregnant doe. We've been watching her for a few weeks, now. She's just about ready to fawn."

"A winter fawn?" Warner said with surprise. "Are you sure? I mean, that doesn't happen often."

Rafford answered, "Come along and see for yourself."

Rafford and Warner walked behind the dogsled and Rafford told his old friend about George Harder and the gun club. Warner was particularly interested in Rafford's description of how they would drive deer and other wildlife from the state lands onto gun club property.

"These guys have built a pretty bad reputation, but we haven't been able to catch them in the act, breaking any laws," Warner said. "Maybe this is our chance."

Tyler stopped the sled and motioned to Rafford and the ranger to be quiet. The doe stood motionless amid the trees about 25 yards ahead of them, looking placidly in their direction. She seemed to relax after a few moments and resumed chewing on some underbrush.

Warner, moving very slowly, pulled his spotting scope from his pocket and took a long look at the doe. "Well, this is a first for me," he whispered. "She's pregnant, alright; that fawn is going to come any day now."

The three of them watched the doe for several minutes, until she walked slowly away and disappeared into the forest.

"She has a nesting area not far from here," Rafford explained to Warner. "She doesn't stray very far, anymore. We usually spot her somewhere nearby."

Warner looked concerned, "If I have my bearings right, the Black Stag property line is just over that rise."

Rafford nodded, "That's one reason we have been watching her. I don't think they know about her, but their nighttime excursions run so close to here, I'm afraid they will scare her out into the open."

"Can you show me the place where they come through the fence?" Warner asked.

"Sure. We better move quickly, though, we don't have much daylight left, and Tyler and I still have a ways to go." Rafford answered. "Hey, where are you staying tonight? Maybe you could have dinner with us?"

"I'm staying with Peter Boggs over at the Raquette Falls ranger cabin. It's a good place to sleep, but Peter can't cook a lick. A real home-cooked meal sounds great! Before we leave, I want to make a note of these coordinates," Warner said as he pulled an electronic Global Positioning System device from his pocket.

While the ranger made his notes of the location, he explained to Tyler how to use the GPS satellites to pinpoint exact map coordinates.

When they reached the broken down sections of fence, Warner paced around the area, looking at the fence line from every angle, and he took several more sets of GPS readings. When he finished, they separated; Warner headed back to where he had left his Jeep and Rafford and Tyler began their trek back to Deer Run.

At dinner that night, Warner entertained everyone with story after story of his experiences as a ranger. He was such a good storyteller, that Rafford could not tell when the facts ended and Travis's imagination took over, embellishing the details. Abigail was not at all flustered about having an unexpected guest for dinner; however, she did seem embarrassed by the ranger's flattery.

"It's true, Mrs. Sherwood; you are something of a legend among the park rangers. You know more about these mountains that most of us do, and you have never hesitated to speak-out when some air-headed politician pretends that he understands what it means to call these mountains, home. They all think they know the Adirondacks, but they don't know bear scat about the mountains! You manage to keep them in line. A few words from you carry more weight than pages of reports and memos from us. I hope you will continue to speak-out; and your children and grandchildren, too," he said looking right at Tyler.

"Enough, Mr. Warner! You are certainly overstating my importance. Besides, I have no desire to be Joan of Arc for the Adirondacks; after all look how it turned out for her!" Abigail said with a sly smile. "Let's leave the dishes – we'll have dessert in the living room; I want to enjoy looking at that beautiful Christmas tree."

"Thank you, Mrs. Sherwood, but I really have to be going. I left my dog with Peter Boggs back at the cabin and I need to get back to be sure he is still OK."

Rafford asked, "You don't think Storm is safe with Peter?"

Warner laughed, "I'm not worried about Storm; it's Peter I need to check on." He turned to Abigail, "Thank you for the delicious dinner, Mrs. Sherwood; it was a real treat. I hope to see you again, sometime."

"I'm glad you were able to join us," Abigail said. "You're welcome here again, anytime, provided you stop calling me Mrs. Sherwood." Then she added, "Any help you can provide with our gun club problem will be greatly appreciated."

Rafford walked outside with Warner. The two of them stood next to the ranger's jeep for several minutes engaged in conversation. When Rafford returned to the house, he found Abigail and Tyler in the living room. The boy was completely entangled in strings of Christmas lights.

"Don't say a word, Rafford Brown," Abigail chided. "Just help Tyler sort out those lights. We'll decorate the tree when Carolyn comes home. But the lights we can do tonight."

The three of them spent the next hour untangling and hanging strings of tiny blue and white lights on the tree. Tyler sat on Rafford's shoulders so he could string the lights around the top of the tree. Abigail supervised mostly, offering what she called 'artistic advice' about where the lights should be placed.

Tyler had the honor of plugging-in the long extension cord and lighting the tree. The delicate lights enveloped the deep green tree like stars scattered about by some distant galaxy. Abigail, Tyler and Rafford, stood for several moments, in silent appreciation, then Rafford lowered his eyes and turned away. He felt a crushing sadness come over him; he was sure it had to show on his face and he did not want them to see. If he had to explain right now, it would be more than he could bear.

Abigail wrapped her arms around Tyler from behind and pulled him close. "This is what I love most about Christmas," she said softly.

"But, Grandma, the tree isn't even decorated yet," Tyler protested.

"It's not the tree, Tyler. It's doing all the little things that we do to celebrate this holy season. These times together, are what make us a family and keep us connected, even with those who can't be here with us. Looking at this tree reminds me of all the other trees that have stood in this room, and of decorating them with your Grandpa and your mother when she was no bigger than you are now. Someday, I hope, you will stand in this room admiring another tree, maybe with your grandchildren, and you will remember this perfectly beautiful tree and this moment. It is what makes us a family – you, your mother, and me and this year, I think we'll have to add Rafford to our extended family."

"Don't forget Uncle Amos," Tyler added.

"No, we can't forget 'Uncle Amos'," Abigail laughed and hugged the boy even tighter against her.

She turned to say something to Rafford and realized that he had left the room.

"Tyler, it's time to get ready for bed. I'll come up and tuck you in, in a few minutes."

She found Rafford in the kitchen, by the window, "Tyler's getting ready for bed," she offered tentatively. "Is something wrong?"

"No, I'm just not very good with family moments," he answered. "I didn't want to intrude."

"Rafford, you never intrude. You belong here – I know that sounds odd after such short time, but you do. It is as if you have always lived here. I don't think of you as a hired hand; you are more like a long-lost relative, come home at last."

Rafford looked at her skeptically.

"Don't look at me like that!" Abigail said. "I'm old, but I'm not dotty, yet. But even if you think I am crazy, would you please humor me? I really would like you to be part of our family for Christmas. It's not a good time of year to be alone; believe me, I know. Besides, Tyler would never understand if you were not included."

At that moment, Tyler's voice rang out from upstairs, "Where is everybody? I'm ready for bed!"

Abigail went upstairs to say goodnight. Rafford sat in the flickering light but still could not bring himself to look directly at the Christmas tree. The aching in his chest had eased some, but he still felt blanketed in stifling sadness. He did not hear Abigail come down the stairs, and when she spoke, it startled him.

"Tyler wants you to come upstairs for a minute. He said he wants to ask you something."

Rafford found Tyler sitting up in bed, Abigail's patchwork quilt pulled up under his arms. "What's up, Tyler? Your grandmother said you wanted to ask me something."

"I was wondering," the boy seemed to be searching for the right words. "When we put the lights on the Christmas tree, you looked really sad. Were you thinking about Casey?"

Rafford took a step back, and looked at the boy in wonder, amazed that he not only noticed his sadness, but he intuitively understood what he was feeling. He did not know what to say.

Before he could answer, Tyler said, "Our tree is really pretty, but I bet they have even prettier Christmas trees in heaven."

As Rafford stood, speechless, Tyler climbed out of bed, walked over and put his arms around Rafford. Rafford rested his hand on Tyler's head, and nodded, but words would not come.

≈

Chapter Sixteen

Rafford crossed the barnyard, his shoulders hunched and his coat collar high against the steady snowfall. Snow had begun falling early Thursday morning and by noon, several inches covered the ground. The storm showed no signs of letting up.

Earlier, Rafford had moved the goats to the barn in spite of their noisy protests. Once they were safely locked away, he placated them with generous rations of feed and water. The chickens never ventured outside the coop that morning. Without the livestock, the barnyard seemed strangely silent, absent the usual noise and commotion. By early afternoon, the thickening blanket of snow muffled even the sound of Rafford's own footsteps.

When he reached the porch, he flopped down in his favorite Adirondack chair. Pulling a worn leather pouch from his coat pocket, he filled the bowl of his gnarled briar pipe, tamped it down and struck a match. After a couple of deep drags, the sweet scent of tobacco hung in the air all around his head. As he settled back in the chair, he marveled at how pipe smoke always smelled so much better than it tasted.

"Mr. Brown," Abigail said from the doorway, "if I had known that you smoked I might have had second thoughts about engaging your services."

Rafford smiled at the teasing tone of her voice, but then he wondered if she might truly object. "I don't smoke often. If you prefer, I can live just fine without it."

"No, that isn't necessary, but please don't smoke around Tyler. Actually, I like the aroma; it reminds me of Roger. His tobacco had a different smell – tinged with vanilla." Abigail stood leaning against the doorjamb, her eyes closed and a faint smile on her lips. "He always smoked a special tobacco that he bought from a shop in Lake Placid. I don't remember the name of the shop, but he loved that tobacco. Whenever he passed anywhere near there, he would stop and restock his supply. Even after he quit smoking, he carried a small pouch of that tobacco in his pocket. Every so often, he would bury his nose in the pouch and breathe deep. He was a man of few vices, but he dearly loved that pipe tobacco."

The conversation waned as each of them stared at the falling snow, lost in private thoughts. Absentmindedly, Rafford hummed a tune.

"What's that song you're humming?" Abigail asked.

"I don't remember the name. It's from a set of Adirondack songs by a musician I met up at Cranberry Lake. I like the words," Rafford answered and then began softly singing, "*In the rushing of the waters, in the whisper of the breeze, in the way the sunlight filters through a canopy of trees. I will always walk beside you; you'll hear me calling low, in the rumble of the thunder, in the hush of falling snow.*"

"That's nice," Abigail said.

Rafford nodded, "He told me he wrote it for his son. The song is about how people eventually go their own way, but some bonds, like the ties between a parent and child, are never broken. I always think of that song when it snows the way it is today; no wind, no noise at all, just a pervasive quiet that seems to absorb every sound; *'the hush of falling snow'*. It's a very peaceful feeling."

Later, at the lunch table, Tyler was anything but peaceful. He could not sit still; he played with his sandwich and fidgeted constantly, annoying Abigail until she seemed ready to explode.

"Tyler! What is wrong with you, today? You have been bouncing off the walls all morning!"

"I don't have anything to do. Just sitting around watching the snow fall is boring," the boy answered.

"Be patient, the storm is supposed to end later today," Rafford said. "I was thinking we should go up and check on the doe, first thing tomorrow morning."

"All right!" Tyler said, full of enthusiasm. "I can't wait to try the sled in all this snow."

"Actually, I think we would do better with snowshoes," Rafford replied. "Over a foot of this light, fluffy snow would be too much for the dogs. Besides, you haven't tried out those snowshoes, yet."

"I don't know how to put them on," Tyler said guiltily. "I tried to figure it out last week, but I couldn't do it."

Rafford laughed, "I know; it can be tough. I remember my first time – the binding on one shoe was too loose so every third or fourth step, my boot would come right out of the snowshoe. The other binding was too tight, so with every step I took, my snowshoe flipped a big spray of snow, straight up the back of my jacket. I nearly froze! Anyway, let's look for a break in the storm this afternoon, so we can test out your snowshoes."

The storm finally eased-up just before sundown, and Rafford and Tyler took advantage of the lull. After a few adjustments and a little instruction, Rafford had Tyler walking from the house to the barn doing what the boy called 'the zombie walk'. He walked stiff-legged, feet spread far apart to keep the snowshoes from banging together.

"Easy does it, Tyler," Rafford said as the boy snagged the tip of his right snowshoe and sprawled in the snow. "It just takes a little practice; use the ski poles for balance."

When the boy was able to move more comfortably through the deep snow, Rafford suggested they go for a walk down toward the river. They started out slowly, with Tyler in front and Rafford following close behind, watching his every move. They pushed their way through the woods, passing under and around tree branches that bent low over the trail, laden down with snow. Tyler did well and only stumbled twice when the tips of his snowshoes caught on underbrush blanketed by the heavy snow.

"Tyler, stop - don't go any farther," Rafford called out.

"Why are we stopping here? I thought we were going down to the river."

"This is the river," Rafford replied. "If you look straight ahead, it's hard to see, but look to either side and you can see the line of the river bank."

Tyler looked both ways, his eyes squinted against the glare, but all he saw was a smooth cover of bright, white snow.

"Is the river frozen?" Tyler asked.

"It's hard to say," Rafford answered. "I would guess that there is just enough ice on top for the snow to cling to; but probably not enough ice to hold our weight. You always have to be careful around rivers in the winter. River water is always moving under the ice. A lake can be covered with a foot of solid ice, but a river coming out of that same lake might have just a thin crust of ice on top because the water underneath is constantly in motion."

Rafford showed Tyler how to pick out the undulations in the snow that marked the river's edge, and then said, "OK, that's the end of today's lesson. Let's head back, but let's bushwhack a new trail to the house, just for fun."

They snaked their way through the woods, weaving around fallen trees, climbing over rocks and other obstacles.

By the time they reached the house, they were both tired. They left the snowshoes on the porch, ready for the next day's hike to Hart Mountain.

The storm had blown itself out before morning leaving behind eighteen inches of fresh powdery snow, and much deeper drifts in some places. Abigail prepared a hearty breakfast –oatmeal with honey and raisins, bran muffins, and lots of coffee and hot chocolate. She packed a thermos of chocolate and a couple of extra muffins for their hike.

"I'll feed the animals after you've gone," she said as Rafford finished his coffee.

He downed the last swallow and answered, "Already done, Abigail. I will run the snowplow when we get back, then maybe we can coax the goats outside for a while. They are not very happy about sharing that stall. I would do it first but..."

"I know," Abigail interrupted. "Your best chance to spot the doe is early morning. The goats will be fine, until you get back."

Tyler gulped down the last of his breakfast, "I'm ready. I'll just get my parka."

Abigail stopped him, "Tyler, for snowshoeing you would do better leaving the heavy coat here; just wear some layers."

Rafford agreed, "Keep your thermal underwear on, then maybe a wool or flannel shirt, then a fleece vest and on top a water-resistant jacket – that green anorak you have would be perfect."

In a few minutes, they were ready to go. Rafford double-checked Tyler's snowshoe bindings, adjusted his daypack and then called to Smokey and Dog. The two dogs were rolling around in the snow near the barn, but they came on the run when he whistled, and the four of them set off, in loose formation.

The rising sun had not yet topped Hart Mountain but the sky glowed in vibrant shades of orange and yellow. A few minutes into their hike, the sun appeared over the mountaintop and lit up the morning.   The view was breathtaking – snow-covered trees, rocks, and mountains shimmered in the morning light under a neon blue sky. Rafford drank it in, savoring the moment; a crystal-clear winter morning always filled him with energy and enthusiasm.

He looked ahead and saw Tyler, head down, laboring to keep up the pace. Rafford feared he would miss the sunrise.

He called to him, "Tyler! Let's stop for a minute and get our bearings."

The boy stopped walking and, after a moment, he looked around, his head moving slowly, his eyes wide, as he scanned the horizon. Rafford smiled broadly, as he watched the boy's reaction.

"I've never..." Tyler began, but he did not finish the sentence.

Rafford nodded, "I know; it's amazing. Sometimes it's hard to get out of a warm bed on a cold winter morning, but when you get a morning like this..." this time Rafford did not finish his sentence.

They walked on, saying little, other than Rafford suggesting an occasional adjustment in their direction.   Finally, they reached the downed birch tree that marked their usual spot for watching the doe.

Crouched in the snow, they peered through the bare tree branches, waiting and watching. Rafford scanned the area carefully, with his binoculars and then handed the glasses to Tyler.

Tyler peered through the glasses for some time and then said, "I don't see her."

"What about tracks? In this soft snow, tracks should be easy to see," Rafford prodded.

"No tracks, either."

"So, if she was in there when the snow started..." Rafford left the sentence for Tyler to finish.

"She must still be in there," the boy said. "So we wait?"

They had waited only a few minutes before Tyler noticed branches moving on the bottom right of the tree. The snow-covered limbs, bent almost to the ground, stirred slightly, shaking off some of the snow. Rafford trained his binoculars on the spot, expecting to see the doe emerge; but it was not the doe.

"It's a dog!" Tyler exclaimed. "What is he doing there and where's the deer?"

"It's not a dog, Tyler, it's a coyote," Rafford said sadly. "Something is not right. I'm going in closer for a look; you stay here."

Before he could move, however, the two dogs caught the scent of the coyote. In one swift move, they leaped over the downed birch tree barking and growling chasing full-steam after the coyote. Rafford did not try to stop them; he knew the coyote was too quick for them and that the dogs would be back soon.

As Rafford stood to go, Tyler said, "I'm coming, too."

"Tyler, coyotes sometimes hunt deer," Rafford explained. "Our doe would have been an easy target. She couldn't run; heck, she could barely walk the last time we saw her. Through the binoculars, I saw some dark splotches that looked like blood on the forelegs of that coyote. Are you sure you want to see what is under the tree?"

The boy's eyes showed his fear, but he firmly said, "Yes, I want to see."

Together, they approached the doe's nesting area carefully, listening for sounds of other coyotes and watching for movement; but all was still. Rafford went straight to the side of the tree from where the coyote had emerged. He lifted the branch, hoping to find the nesting area empty. Instead, he saw the remains of a deformed fawn's body, lying on a patch of snow and pine needles stained dark with blood.

Before Rafford could say anything, he heard Tyler gasp; the boy was peering under Rafford's arm at the dead fawn. Tyler turned away quickly.

"I'll kill him!" Tyler said. "I'm going after that coyote, and I'm going to kill him, dead!"

Rafford put his arm around the boy's shoulders and spoke softly, "Tyler, it's okay. That is what coyotes do, they cull the weak and sick and scavenge the bodies of the ones that have died. It's their job."

"But the fawn never had a chance," Tyler said as tears filled his eyes.

"This fawn didn't have a chance, anyway. He was deformed; he may have even been stillborn. I'm as disappointed as you are, but this is all part of life in the mountains."

"Did the coyote kill the doe, too?" Tyler asked.

"That's a good question. I don't know where she is; let's keep looking and see what we find."

On the backside of the tree, hidden behind a decaying tree trunk and heavy underbrush, Tyler found deer tracks.

"Rafford, over here!" he called.

Rafford got down on one knee and looked closely at the marks in the deep snow. "Those are deer tracks, alright. It's hard to be sure in all this snow, but I think there is more than one set of tracks here."

They followed the trail for several minutes. Rafford regularly stopped to scan the woods with the binoculars. He wanted to find the doe, but he did not want to scare her off. She seemed to be moving consistently upward, toward the higher terrain, on a line roughly parallel with the fence that separated Abigail's land from the gun club. The tracks moved steadily in the same direction, as though the doe knew where she was headed, and Rafford feared that if they frightened her, she would change direction and that could be trouble.

Finally, the tracks disappeared into cluster of spruce trees. Rafford and Tyler settled in behind a large boulder and waited; watching through the binoculars for any sign of movement.

Tyler started to say something, but Rafford put his finger to his lips, and shook his head no. If the doe was in there, the slightest sound could scare her away.

Just then, the doe slipped out from under the tree and took a few tentative steps toward the spot where Rafford and Tyler waited. She flared her nostrils, sniffing at the air, and then she moved her head slowly, side-to-side, searching for any sign of danger. Rafford watched her through the glasses, relieved to see that she seemed to be unharmed and that she bore no signs of a fight with the coyote. Then the branch behind her moved, ever so slightly, and the smallest fawn Rafford had ever seen crawled through the snowdrift until he brushed up against her side. The fawn stood, legs trembling slightly, and nuzzled against his mother's belly.

Rafford handed the binoculars to Tyler, and whispered, "Looks like she has a fawn, after all. No noise!"

They watched the two deer for several minutes, taking turns with the field glasses. Then, in an instant, the doe and her fawn darted back under the tree branches, as if something had frightened them.

"What happened?" Tyler said softly.

"I don't know," Rafford replied, "but now that we know that they are alright, it's time for us to leave. We had better find Smokey and Dog and head back home."

"Rafford, if that is her fawn, then what fawn did we see before?"

"I suspect that she had twins, but that only one fawn was born alive; that would explain what we saw before and it would also explain why this fawn is so small," Rafford said. "Come on, let's go find those dogs."

"Well, well, well, we meet again!"

Startled, Rafford snapped his head around toward the voice. George Harder stood only a few steps away dressed in full winter camouflage; even his snowshoes were painted gray and white. Rafford noticed that he carried a rifle with a scope, slung over one shoulder.

"Harder," Rafford said loudly, "and on snowshoes, too! What happened did your snowmobile run out of gas?"

Harder smirked at him, "You can save the stage voice, Brown. I already saw the doe – and her fawn, too. You know, I've heard about winter fawns, but in more than forty years in these mountains, that is the first one I have ever seen."

"Let me be the first to remind you, Harder," Rafford said, "that deer is on private property – and so are you. You're trespassing, so why don't you head back to your side of the line, and leave all of us alone."

"Trespassing?" Harder replied with feigned innocence, "why Rafford, old friend, with all this snow, it's so hard to know just where that property line runs."

In one smooth and practiced motion, Harder swung the rifle from his shoulder and brought it into firing position. He pointed the gun toward the tree that sheltered the deer, sighting through the scope.

"Harder!" Rafford shouted.

"This scope brings everything close enough to touch..."

Dog and Smokey appeared suddenly.   Snarling and growling they charged out of the trees and ran straight at Harder. Surprised, he jerked the rifle around and the gun went off, firing a single shot into the air. The dogs stopped dead, stunned by the sound. The recoil from the rifle knocked Harder off balance and he fell backwards into the snow.

The dogs started toward Harder again. Rafford called, firmly, "Smokey! Dog! Whoa!" and the dogs stopped in their tracks.

Harder struggled back to his feet, his face flushed and his eyes filled with rage as he pointed a finger at the dogs. "You keep those flea-bitten mongrels away from me, Brown, or your scraggly deer won't be the only things in my gun sights."

"You and your threats are not welcome here, Harder," Rafford said evenly.

Harder started to say something in response, but did not. Instead, he glared at them, then turned around and headed back toward the gun club.

Rafford watched him walk away until he was completely out of sight. Then he pulled his trail diary from his daypack, and wrote down a full description of the doe's new nesting area. He wished that he had Rick Grundy's GPS to record the exact coordinates, but he did the best he could with his map and compass. He was sure that she would not return to the earlier spot so, if they were to find her and the fawn again, this would be the place to start looking.

Back at Deer Run, Tyler told Abigail everything. She listened patiently and occasionally glanced at Rafford for confirmation. When the boy described the confrontation with George Harder, her face clouded.

"I'm going to call Curtis, and tell him that Harder is trespassing, again."

"Stay calm, Abigail," Rafford cautioned. "You know the sheriff isn't able to do anything about him crossing the property line, unless we can prove that he is hunting on your land."

Abigail interrupted, "So we just wait for him to shoot that doe or her fawn? I won't let that happen and I can't stand the thought of him roaming around, out there, in Roger's woods."

"I know, but right now, all we can do is keep watching until we have solid proof, enough proof to press charges," Rafford said with resignation.

Abigail, sighed and then smiled at Tyler, "Well, you've got a lot to tell your mother when she comes home, tomorrow."

Book III – Home Again

I make my home above the snowline
Where the mountains brush
the clouds from the sky.
Home to beaver, fox and the bear
Where brother eagle learned to fly.
From the heights
of my mountain hideaway
I can see exactly who I am.
As if a part of me was born from the land
Up here I'm free to be my own man.
O Adirondacks!
I love your mountain lakes,
rivers and streams
O Adirondacks!
Mountains of my dreams.

- O Adirondacks
© William Delia

⋙⋘

Chapter Seventeen

C arolyn felt uneasy all the way back from Austin. Christmas was just four days away and holiday travelers filled the flight from Austin to Albany. The plane had been three hours late leaving Austin because of a storm front in the Midwest and most of the passengers had taken advantage of the delay by seeking some holiday spirit in the airport cocktail lounge. Carolyn had not joined the celebration; instead, she had nervously paced the airport corridors for most of the delay. The last thing she needed, right now, was more time to kill; more time to think about her dilemma.

Over the past three weeks, she had spent more solitary time, thinking and wondering, than she could ever remember. Day after day, she sat by the telephone at Zoe's house, hoping for job interview callbacks. She desperately wanted to do well on the interviews, to find and win the right job, even though she still had doubts about moving to Austin. She longed for the personal validation that a good job offer would give. Even if she decided not to move here, her instincts about Austin would be born out – if only someone wanted her.

As tough as the days had been, the evenings with Zoe were just the opposite. They stayed up late every night, laughing together and sharing secrets in the kind of late-night conversation that happens only with a true friend. She had almost forgotten how good it felt to have that kind of friendship.

Now, sitting on the plane, she leaned her head against the bulkhead staring forlornly out the window. She was going home after nearly a month of anticipating and agonizing, but she still had no idea what she was going to do. She had received two jobs offers in Austin. One she had rejected outright as too corporate for her; she could not bring herself to use her education and skills to enrich the oil company with the worst environmental record in the country.

"No matter how well you gift wrap your garbage, it still stinks when the bag breaks," Zoe had surmised.

Carolyn felt the same way, but she lacked Zoe's descriptive language.

"It's a gift," Zoe would say.

The second offer still tempted her, even though the salary was less than she was making now. She rationalized that the lower cost of living in Texas would offset most of the lost wages and the up side of joining a firm on the rise made the offer worth serious consideration. Unfortunately, long, hard thought was not working. The more she thought about what to do, the more she agonized. Her weary mind overflowed with uncertainties about the job, about moving from Boston all the way to Texas, and about where she could make the best home for Tyler. In the end, Tyler meant more to her than anything else.

Yesterday, on her last day in Austin, she had made up her mind to accept the offer. It was a good opportunity. She would be in on the ground floor and she told herself that Tyler would learn to love, or at least tolerate, living in Texas. Even if he did not love Texas, he would certainly love Zoe. Zoe would be like a sister to Carolyn and a favorite aunt to Tyler.

Last night, Zoe and Carolyn had gone clubbing, "trolling the night spots" in Zoe's parlance. Austin's music scene is legendary, and Zoe loved to dance. Carolyn made her announcement over Texas-sized margaritas at the Avaricious Armadillo.

"Zoe, I've decided to take the job at Sweetman Communications. We're coming to Texas! Wahoo!" she announced with all the enthusiasm she could muster.

"Well, it's about time you made up your mind, girl! This is truly a red-letter day; it looks like things could really work out, for both of us!" Zoe reached across the table and embraced her; then they clinked glasses and each took a huge gulp.

Carolyn wiped the pale green froth and salt from her lips and said, "I want to thank you; I don't know what I would have done these past weeks without you. You always did see things clearer than I did. You know me – I always have to hedge my bets. Anyway, I figure that even if the job is a total bust, at least I'll be with my best friend, ever. Wait until you see Tyler – he is really something special."

"I can't wait to see him, again. I just hope you two make it back before I leave for California," Zoe paused with a silly grin on her face, waiting for Carolyn to react.

"California?" Carolyn said. "You're going to California? What's in California?"

"Only my future, I hope!" Zoe answered excitedly. "I've been busting at the seams to tell you - Stewie called me at work, today. He wants me to come to live with him in San Jose! His job is really working out and..."

Zoe kept talking but Carolyn heard little of her plans to move west and eventually become Mrs. Stewart Danielson. Her head was spinning. She wanted to be happy for her friend, but Zoe's announcement had her totally confused. Austin lost a lot of its attraction without Zoe, and deciding to move across the country because of an old college friendship suddenly seemed foolish and shallow.

"Hey, are you OK?"

Carolyn heard the voice over the hum of the airplane's engines. The woman in the seat next to her was looking at her with concern.

"Are you OK?" the woman said again, offering Carolyn a tissue.

Only then, did Carolyn feel the tears on her cheeks. She took the tissue and dabbed at her eyes, before answering.

"Thanks. I was thinking...," she stammered. "I didn't even realize I was crying."

"It's the time of year," the woman said. "Everything seems more stressful, more emotional, around the holidays."

Carolyn nodded, hoping her silent agreement would end the conversation. The woman was about her own age and seemed nice enough, but Carolyn just was not up for small talk with a stranger.

"Are you traveling home for Christmas?" the woman asked, then without waiting for Carolyn's answer, she continued, "I'm going home to Pittsburgh for the first time in seven years. Talk about stress; half the people I care about, probably won't even remember me and the other half will for-sure wish that I had stayed away. I can't blame them; they have a right to feel that way."

"So, why go back? I mean, if that's the way it's going to be, why do it?" Carolyn asked.

"Pittsburgh is still home," the woman said with resignation, "besides, where else would I go? Home is home, right?"

"I guess so," Carolyn said tentatively.

"I guess so?" the woman mocked. "Darlin', everybody's gotta have a home – like it or not. We all call someplace home; where's yours?"

"You mean a specific place?"

The woman's mouth dropped open, "Yeah, a place. What else would it be?"

Carolyn chose her words carefully, "Well, right now, I really don't know. Home used to be where my parents live, in upstate New York. For the past few years, I've been living in Boston with my son, Tyler– but, you know, it never really felt like home. Now, I'm thinking of moving to Texas, so maybe that will be home. At this point in my life, home isn't a particular place; it's anywhere that I am with Tyler. He's the most important part of home to me."

The woman nodded knowingly, "I can understand that – I have a 12 year-old daughter. But, if your home is with your son, where is *his* home?"

Carolyn did not understand, "What do you mean?"

"I mean, if he was here and I asked him where his home is, what would he say? You know how kids are, they see things pretty clearly, whether we want them to, or not. So, where would he say home is?"

The woman waited, but Carolyn did not answer.

"Maybe you should ask him?" the woman suggested.

"What would your daughter say," Carolyn challenged, resentful of the woman's attitude.

The woman's face clouded over, "If I asked her, she would say that her home is in Pittsburgh - with her grandmother, if she would even bother to answer me. I haven't seen her or even spoken to her since she was four years old; they all said it would be better for her," the emptiness in her voice surrounded them both. "I would give anything to be with her again. I just hope it's not too late."

The woman turned away from Carolyn and closed her eyes. Carolyn moved her mouth but could not speak. She wanted to know more about the woman and her daughter, but she could not begin to find the words to ask. How could a mother live, separated from her child like that? Some days she felt so connected to Tyler that she knew she could not draw even one more breath without seeing him. Just knowing that he was there with her, helped her tolerate everything else. She would always feel she was home as long as they were together; but was it the same for him? She wondered how Tyler would answer the woman's question. Where would he call home? It troubled her for the rest of the flight that she did not know the answer. What troubled her even more was that she was afraid to ask him the question.

The plane touched down in Albany with a light snow drifting across the runway. Carolyn stopped at a pay phone outside the baggage claim area and dialed her mother's number. Tyler answered the telephone and she was relieved that he sounded happy to hear her voice.

"Hi, Mom! Rafford and I saw the fawn yesterday! He is so little he looks like a toy! Rafford says he looks healthy, but he doesn't know if he will make it through the winter. Tomorrow Rafford is going to the Agway for a salt lick – deer need salt, did you know that?" Before she could answer he started talking again, "Anyway, Rafford and I are going to put the salt lick near the doe's nest, so they will be sure to find it. Then we can..."

"Tyler!" Carolyn said, louder than she intended. Moderating her voice she continued, "You can tell me everything, as soon as I get home. I'm at the airport in Albany, right now, so I will be there soon. I need to speak with your grandmother for a moment, OK?"

"OK," Tyler said and Carolyn could hear the disappointment in his voice.

"Tyler," she said quickly, "I really do want to hear all about the fawn when I get there, OK?"

"Sure, Mom," the boy answered. "Here's Grandma."

"Carolyn? Hi, where are you?" Abigail asked.

"Hi, Mom; I'm at the airport in Albany, waiting for my bags," Carolyn said. "I should be on the road pretty soon. Is it snowing there?"

"Just a few flurries; the roads should be good but be sure to drive carefully."

"I'll be careful. Don't wait supper for me; I probably won't get there until nearly eight o'clock," Carolyn said.

After another word of caution from Abigail, they said goodbye.

Carolyn was looking forward to the long drive back to Deer Run. It would be a refreshing change after the tiring flight and the emotional roller coaster of the past several days. Driving snow-slicked roads through the mountains required complete concentration and she knew that kind of concentration would block-out the nagging questions that had dogged her for weeks.

The snow-covered forests of upstate New York were a welcome change after the wide-open brown monotony of Texas. Winter in the mountains could be bitter and harsh, but few sights were as beautiful. The rolling horizon of evergreen and snow was broken only by random stands of white birch trees or sugar maples recently stripped of their brilliant autumn yellows and reds.

Driving north, as the sun slipped behind the mountains, Carolyn spotted a bird circling slowly over the highway. Hawks frequently perched on bare-limbed hardwoods along this stretch of the road, but this bird looked too large to be a hawk. She thought that it could be one of the bald eagles that regularly wintered near Conklingville Dam. She longed for a closer look - nothing compares to the sight of an eagle on the wing - but tonight the road demanded her full attention.

After more than an hour and a half of two-lane highway, she rolled up the long grade leading into the village of Speculator. She stopped at Charlie John's market for gas and a cup of coffee. The night air, tinged with the familiar rich aroma of pine trees and wood-smoke, brushed icily against her cheeks. Light from a million stars and a nearly-full moon set the December sky aglow. The stars sparked and glistened on cold, clear winter nights in the mountains; their light seemingly purer and more brilliant than any other time of year. Carolyn stood gazing at the sky until she felt her eyes tearing in the cold night air.

The road on the final leg of the drive, from Speculator to Deer Run, was completely clear. She had driven Route 30 a thousand times and she knew every bump and turn in the highway. As she relaxed, her thoughts slowly returned to the decision she must make. The confusion, self-doubt and anxiety that she had felt on the plane abruptly vanished. She realized that something about this place, these mountains, always helped her know what to do. By the time she turned the Volvo into the long driveway to Deer Run, she had no doubt about her decision.

Tyler came running and reached the car, even before she could open the door. Carolyn hugged him and held him close. This was the longest time they had ever been separated and she discovered that she had missed him even more than she had realized.

Abigail called from the porch, "Come inside, you two, before you freeze!"

The three of them sat at the kitchen table while Carolyn ate the dinner that Abigail had insisted on saving for her. Tyler talked non-stop, while she ate, telling her everything that had happened while she had been gone. Mostly, though, he talked about Dog, the fawn and dogsledding. The only way she could get him to stop talking was to promise that she would go with him to see the fawn in the morning.

The change in Tyler amazed her. The shy hesitant ten-year-old that she had left here only a few weeks ago had been transformed. Tyler never stopped smiling as he told her about his adventures. In the past, he would have been self-conscious, answering her questions with two or three word sentences. Now he talked so fast and incessantly that his words seemed to run together in one continuous stream. He described everything in elaborate detail, laughing out-loud at times and, at other times, speaking in tones far too serious for any ten year-old. She also noticed that he included Rafford in nearly every sentence.

Carolyn and Abigail had tea in the living room after Tyler had gone upstairs to get ready for bed. The subject of moving to Texas had not yet been mentioned; not by anyone.

"I can't get over the change in Tyler," Carolyn said, shaking her head. "It's like he grew up three years in three weeks."

"I know what you mean," Abigail answered. "Every day has been a surprise; I never knew what would happen next. He's a good boy, Carolyn; you should be very proud of him."

"He certainly seems to be taken with Rafford. It seemed like every other sentence began or ended with 'Rafford'."

Abigail nodded in agreement, "Rafford has been a God-send for both of us. Everything is different – better – since he arrived here. Why, he's even made Amos Kreal nearly tolerable!"

"Tyler never asked about Texas," Carolyn said. "You haven't asked either, Mother."

"Perry Mason always said, 'never ask a witness a question unless you know what the answer will be'," she said with a smile. "I don't know what you are going to tell me, but I am afraid I won't like the decision."

"I had an interesting conversation with a woman on the plane, today. She asked me where my home was – and I couldn't give her an answer. Then she asked me what Tyler would say, if I asked him where he would call home." Carolyn paused, gazing at the fireplace, and then continued, "I couldn't answer that question, either. For so long, Mom, I knew this place was my home. Even now, when I get close to Deer Run, I feel like I'm coming home. My problem is that I'm still looking for a home of my own to take its place. I hope that Texas will be that place."

"So, you're going to Austin?" the disappointment echoed in Abigail's voice.

Carolyn nodded, "I've been offered a good job, with real upside potential. Austin is a great town with lots to do. Tyler and I will be happy, there. Besides, I can't stand the thought of going back to Boston. Now, I just need to find the right time to tell Tyler."

"Right time or not, I think you just told him," Abigail said, motioning toward the stairs.

Tyler came down the stairs two at a time and marched purposefully into the room. Carolyn quickly tried to gather her thoughts while trying to read the expression on the boy's face.

"Tyler Morgan! Were you eavesdropping on your Grandmother and me?"

The boy faced her, trembling with emotion. Carolyn could not tell if he was ready to cry or to explode in rage. When he spoke, however, his words carried a sense of urgency, but not the angst that showed on his face.

"Mom, I don't want to go to Texas," he said firmly. "Please, don't make me go."

"Tyler, we have been through all of this before," Carolyn said. "I have to decide what's best for us, and right now, I've decided that we are moving to Texas. Just give it a chance, Ty, and you will like it there. You'll make lots of new friends and we'll be able to live in a house of our own – no more upstairs apartments for us!"

"But, Mom!" Tyler interrupted, pleading.

"Don't 'but Mom' me, Tyler," Carolyn cut him off. "I know it will be a big change. I know you want to stay in Boston; you know it there - your school and friends and everything. You will get to know Austin, too, and after a while you'll like it there as much as you like Boston – maybe more."

"Mom! Ask me!" the boy pleaded, "Ask me where I think home is. You said you didn't know what I would say, so ask me!"

"Not now, Tyler," Carolyn answered.

"Mom, you don't understand! I don't want to go to Texas – but I don't want to go back to Boston, either. I want to stay here! This is home for me, more than anywhere else in the world. This is home!"

Carolyn could not answer; she opened her mouth but no words came out. Tyler had caught her completely off-guard. Here - he wants to stay here! Her mind raced through all the possible responses, but none seemed to fit. It had never occurred to her that her son would choose to grow up here, in the same place where she had grown up.

Abigail had been watching, silently, but seeing Carolyn's distress, she stepped in, "Tyler, this is not the time. Besides, you know better than to listen-in on other people's conversations. Your mother and I need time to talk, and you need to be patient. When the time is right, your mother will talk with you about all of this. Now say goodnight and go to bed."

"But, Grandma," the boy protested.

"Tyler," Carolyn said, "Grandma is right. We need time to talk and I'm not ready to discuss this with you, right now. So, go to bed, and we'll talk later – I promise."

"But, Mom, later will be too late!"

Carolyn held up her hand, "Tyler, stop! I promise I won't make a final decision until you and I have had a long talk. OK? Now, go upstairs and go to sleep."

The two women sat in silence for several minutes, waiting for Tyler to settle into bed. When they could no longer hear him rustling around upstairs, Abigail spoke, "I'm sorry, dear. I had no idea."

"You should have, Mother," Carolyn said, "and I should have, too. The way he went on about everything; the dogs, the sledding, the deer, Amos, Rafford. This place must feel like a great adventure to him."

"Is that so bad?" Abigail asked. "I mean, is it so bad for a ten-year-old boy to feel like his life is an adventure?"

"Of course not, but you and I know, it won't last – it can't. It's like the difference between going somewhere on vacation and living life there every day. Vacations are more fun but they always end. Real life, however..." she let her voice trail off, regretfully. "What in the world am I going to do?"

Chapter Eighteen

Rafford was working in the hayloft when Tyler came into the barn carrying a battered old milk pail.

"Tyler," Rafford called, "I'm up here!"

"I've got breakfast for you," the boy answered. "I'll bring it up."

Tyler confidently climbed the ladder to the loft, keeping a firm grip on the handle of the bucket.

"Your grandmother is always afraid that someone is going hungry," Rafford said with a smile as he took the bucket from the boy.

"She said you missed breakfast."

Rafford nodded as he unpacked a sausage and egg sandwich, "I did. I wanted to get an early start on the chores. There is a lot to do before we go to see the fawn. Besides, I saw your Mom's car and thought it might be a little busy in the kitchen this morning."

Tyler looked away from him and said quietly, "She came home last night."

"You don't sound very happy about that."

The boy did not say anything. He sat with his knees pulled up to his chest and fidgeted with the laces on his boots.

"Here, have part of my muffin. As usual, your grandmother packed more food than any one person can eat."

Rafford figured that the boy would tell him what was bothering him, eventually, but only when he was ready. The two of them sat quietly while Rafford finished his sandwich and Tyler picked at the blueberry muffin. As Rafford took down the last of his coffee, the boy shifted his position and looked at him.

"Why don't you like my Mom?" Tyler asked softly.

Rafford was taken aback by his question. "What makes you think I don't like her?"

"I don't know. I guess it's because whenever she is around, you stay away," the boy answered.

"I don't really know your mother, Tyler," Rafford said. "We got off to a bad start – remember that first day? I don't think she feels right about me being here. I'm sure she's a good person, and if we got to know each other a little better, we would probably get along just fine. Tyler, something else is bothering you this morning. What is it?"

"Mom decided that we are going to move to Texas," he said with sadness heavy in his voice.

"So, she found a new job," Rafford said. "You knew that was why she went there, right? I mean, that was the whole idea – she would go to Austin, find a new job and you two would move there to live. Have you ever been to Texas?"

The boy shook his head.

"Well, it's a great place. The cities are just like cities everywhere, but the countryside is amazing. There is wide-open space everywhere, with nothing but oil wells and tumbleweeds. I've seen Texas and I've seen Boston, and if I were your age, I think I would pick Texas," Rafford said with as much enthusiasm as he could muster.

"Hello, up there!" Amos Kreal called from the open barn door. "I hear we have a new fawn in the woods!"

While the three of them worked around the barn, Amos chattered, non-stop, about his trip to Burlington and his daughter. Rafford knew that he and Tyler had left some things unsaid, but they would have to wait.

Amos kept up his stories until the chores were finished. The last thing they did was load a salt lick into the back of the pickup and pack snowshoes for everyone. Smokey and Dog eagerly hopped into the back of the truck, not waiting for an invitation.

"Carolyn! Welcome back," Amos called when the two women appeared on the porch. "How was your trip? You look lovelier than ever!"

"Why, thank you, 'Uncle Amos'. You're looking well, too," Carolyn said mischievously then she turned and smiled at Rafford, "Good morning, Mr. Brown."

Rafford's face flushed as he stammered a reply. He was struck dumb by how pretty Carolyn was; she was striking even dressed in a ski jacket and worn woolen trousers. Distracted and confused by these new thoughts about Carolyn, he did not hear Abigail speak to him.

She spoke again, louder this time, "Rafford! Are we ready to go?"

He snapped his head around and realized that everyone was looking at him, "Uh, yes, let's go."

Carolyn and Abigail climbed in the cab. Rafford flipped the keys to Amos and then he climbed in the back with Tyler and the dogs. The truck rolled along slowly, pushing through the new-fallen snow and bouncing over ruts and frost heaves. After only a few minutes they reached the large pile of snow that marked the end of the road; they would go the rest of the way on foot.

Everyone strapped on snowshoes except Carolyn who said, "I haven't been on snowshoes in years; I think I'll carry mine."

"Suit yourself," Abigail replied, "but you're taking a chance. We've had a lot of snow already, and the drifts are pretty deep. Just be sure to step where we step."

They set off single file with Rafford leading and breaking the trail for the others. He carried the salt lick on his back while Tyler, walking right behind him, carried Rafford's daypack and field glasses. Abigail, Carolyn and Amos followed. Carolyn was careful to walk in the other's footsteps, stepping only where their snowshoes had packed down the top layer of fresh snow covering the trail. After walking at a steady pace for about 10 minutes, Rafford signaled for everyone to wait while he left the trail and set the salt lick in a small clearing in the woods.

"Why leave it here?" Carolyn asked.

"From this point forward the trail moves closer to the gun club property line. The deer will find it here and maybe that will keep them further from danger," Rafford answered.

Carolyn nodded, knowingly, and smiled at him. Two smiles in one day, he thought.

They walked on and soon approached the place where they had seen the doe and her fawn. Rafford held his finger to his lips signaling the others to remain quiet. He did not know if the doe was still there, but he expected that she would stay nearby since the fawn was still only a few days old. If they were here, she would be very protective of her fawn and could be easily frightened.

They crouched in the snow behind the branches of a downed birch tree. Tyler showed Abigail and Carolyn where to look for the deer. They waited for nearly an hour, but saw no sign of the doe or her fawn.

As Amos passed around a thermos of hot chocolate and some of Abigail's muffins, Rafford whispered to him, "I'm going to circle downwind; maybe I can get a better angle."

Carolyn watched Rafford go, then moved closer to Amos and said in a hushed voice, "Amos, I want to thank you for what you have done for Tyler. I cannot believe how much he changed while I was gone. I have never seen him so sure of himself. It's hard to believe that a boy could grow-up that much in such a short time. Mom told me how you have been with him, over the past few weeks, teaching him how to handle the dogs. I can tell how much that dogsled means to him. Thank you." She leaned closer and kissed the old man on the cheek.

Amos gave a shy smile and said, "Have you seen him run the dogsled, yet? He's very good; both of the dogs respond to him." He paused thoughtfully, and then continued, "Carolyn, I have truly enjoyed teaching the boy about the sled and all, but you need to thank Rafford for the changes in the boy. He truly cares about Tyler and he is much more patient and encouraging than I could ever be. It's obvious that Tyler looks up to him, just watch the two of them together, you'll see. Heck, I'm just a sidekick, you know, the silly old 'uncle' along for the ride and for comic relief. Rafford is the one who really made the difference. That sweet kiss that you gave me – it belongs to him."

"Maybe you're right," she answered. "I have noticed..."

Before she could finish the sentence, Rafford rejoined them.

Tyler spoke first, "Did you see them? Did you see the fawn?"

Rafford nodded, "Yes. They are both there, under the tree branches. The fawn looked restless, so if we wait a little longer they may come out into the open."

Tyler took the field glasses from Rafford and went back to watching the tree where the doe and fawn were hiding. Amos moved nearer to Rafford.

"What's wrong? Did you see something else?" the old man asked.

Rafford nodded, "Snowshoe tracks -- fresh snowshoe tracks. Someone was here, I'm guessing, early this morning."

"Harder?" Amos asked.

"I don't know. I looked around for other signs, but all I saw were snowshoe tracks, all made by the same person."

Just then, Tyler whispered, excitedly, "Rafford! Here they come!"

The doe and her tiny fawn slipped out from under the tree branches. She stood still, sniffing the air, her enormous brown eyes wide and searching. After a few moments, she walked slowly toward a small pile of green branches, with the fawn following close behind. The doe sniffed the branches and then nibbled at the leaves while the fawn imitated her every move.

Rafford muttered under his breath, "Well, I'll be..."

Tyler handed the binoculars to his mother and pointed toward the deer, before he quietly slid over next to Rafford and said, "I don't understand. Where did those branches come from? All of the trees around here have been stripped bare."

"You're right, Tyler. The doe stayed very close to this area over the past few weeks, and she has already eaten everything she could reach."

"So, someone put those branches there?" the boy concluded.

Rafford nodded, "I spotted some snowshoe tracks, over there. Someone was here, recently, probably this morning. I'm guessing they left the branches."

"But, who?" Tyler asked.

"I don't know; maybe someone who cares about them or maybe someone who wants to be sure they stay around here. In a few days, the fawn will be strong enough that they will probably leave this place and, hopefully, wander deeper into the forest – on state-owned land – where they will be safe. Until then, we'll stay close and check on them every day. If someone else is coming around, we'll see who it is."

The five of them took turns with the field glasses for nearly an hour, admiring the doe and her winter fawn. Finally, Abigail motioned to the others that it was time to leave and they quietly slipped away from the fallen tree, and headed back. When they were a safe distance from the deer, Rafford stopped.

"Tyler," Rafford called, "would you lead everyone back to the truck? I want to walk the fence line. I'll catch up with you."

"Okay," the boy answered as he moved to the head of the line. "Be careful."

"I'll be fine – in fact, I will probably be at the truck before you are," Rafford said, smiling.

"I'll come with you," Carolyn said.

"No, that's not necessary," Rafford said quickly. "I'm going to bushwhack through the woods..."

"Mr. Brown," Carolyn said firmly, "you forget I was raised on this land. Bushwhacking a trail is nothing new to me."

Reluctantly, Rafford relented, "Right. Well, at least put on your snowshoes."

"I will be fine. The snow is firm and snowshoes will just slow me down. Let's go."

Rafford shrugged his shoulders and set off through the woods toward the fence that separated them from the gun club. The snow was soft under the trees, where they walked; the shelter of the trees protected the snow from the constant melt and freeze that came with each day's sun. Rafford moved steadily forward, picking a line through the underbrush, around the rocks and downed trees. He looked back several times to check on Carolyn who was walking in his footsteps but struggling in snow halfway up to her knees. When she caught him looking at her, she quickly gave him a "thumbs-up" sign. She is stubborn, Rafford thought, but he had to admire her determination.

They approached a large boulder that rested only a few paces from the fence line. Rafford circled the boulder to the north but just as the fence came into view, he heard a muffled cry from Carolyn. He turned to find her standing nearly waist deep in drifted snow. She was tipped forward, her face brushing the snow, and her right leg bent awkwardly up behind her.

He stifled a laugh, but could not keep from smiling. As he watched, she raised up just enough to wipe a hand across her face.

When she saw him smiling at her she said, "OK, you've had your laugh. Now help me get out of here."

"Actually, I didn't laugh, yet," Rafford managed to say before he broke into raucous laughter.

It took serious effort from both of them but, in a few moments, Carolyn was sitting on top of the boulder brushing the snow from her clothes, as Rafford adjusted her snowshoes.

"Rafford," she said, "I want to thank you for what you have done for Tyler. The change in him is remarkable, and everyone tells me that it's because of you."

"No thanks needed," he answered. "Tyler is a great kid. The truth is he probably helped me more than I helped him."

"Well, thank you anyway," Carolyn said. "I can see now that you being here has been a good thing – for my mother and for Tyler, too. So I want to apologize for being so unfriendly."

"You don't need to apologize or thank me. Abigail has been wonderful to me; she gave me a job for the winter, and I'm just trying to repay her kindness."

Rafford paused for a moment, then continued, cautiously, "It's probably none of my business, but this morning Tyler seemed pretty put-off about moving to Texas. You might –"

Carolyn interrupted, "I know, but he'll be fine once we are settled and he makes some new friends. Please don't encourage him about this; I will take care of everything."

Rafford wanted to say more but decided not to push. Instead, he got to his feet and said, "We'd better go."

Carolyn stumbled a few steps on the snowshoes but then remembered how to keep her feet farther apart and the snowshoe tips up. By the time they reached the fence line, she was moving comfortably. They followed the fence for several minutes before they came to the first cut in the fencing. Rafford looked around for telltale snowmobile tracks, but found none.

"I still don't understand," Carolyn said, "why is there barbed wire here? In fact, now that I think about it, I don't ever remember any fence here, at all. Did you put this fence here?"

"No, I didn't put it here," Rafford answered, "but your mother wants me to keep it up."

"Is that the gun club land over there," she asked. Not waiting for an answer, she said, "Is there a problem with the gun club? They have always been good neighbors."

"You probably should ask Abigail about that," Rafford said.

"I'm asking you," she said firmly. "What is going on?"

Rafford hesitated, and then said, "The new owners of the gun club have their own idea of what makes a good neighbor. They've been running hunting parties onto your mother's land – even onto state land. Apparently, one of them mistakenly took a shot at Smokey a few months ago. Abigail had the fence put up to try to discourage them, but it hasn't worked."

"This has been going on for months?" Carolyn said. "She never told me."

"We better get going. I'll come back with some tools and fix this tomorrow," Rafford said.

He started walking, relieved that Carolyn followed without pressing him for any more details. He did not want to be caught in the middle between Abigail and Carolyn, again.

Carolyn raised the subject of the gun club at dinner that night. "Mom, I was surprised to see barbed wire on the property. Daddy always said he didn't ever want to see barbed wire in the Adirondacks."

"Well, times change," Abigail said. "If your father was still alive, he would understand."

"Rafford said there are new owners at the gun club," Carolyn said tentatively.

"Oh, and what else did Rafford say?" Abigail answered Carolyn but she looked straight at Rafford.

"Nothing," Carolyn said quickly. "But I noticed the fence was cut in a couple of places, so I wondered if there was a problem with the club."

Rafford stood up and said, "Tyler, would you help me with the dishes? Your mother and grandmother need time to talk. We'll be in the kitchen if you need us."

"You don't have to leave," Abigail said, but Rafford and Tyler had already left the room.

"Please, Mom, tell me what's going on," Carolyn pleaded.

Over the next few minutes, Abigail told Carolyn the whole story. She told her about her conflicts with the new owners of the gun club and she told her how George Harder had become a special thorn in her side. She also told her about Rodney Paige and a mysterious offer to buy Deer Run. She had no proof, but she was sure the gun club owners were behind that, too. She didn't mention the new land-use restrictions; she thought that would be too much pressure on Carolyn.

"Now, that poor deer and her little fawn are right in the middle of all this, too," Abigail concluded.

"Mom, that deer is the least of your concerns," Carolyn said. "You can't keep fighting these people by yourself."

"I know," Abigail responded. "Thank God that Rafford came along when he did. They aren't so quick to try to push me around with him here."

"What are you going to do when winter is over and he leaves?" asked Carolyn.

"I don't know," Abigail answered. "Maybe he will stay on."

"Mom, be serious. I mean, he seems like a nice man, but you can't hang all your hopes on a drifter you've known for only a few weeks."

"Well, Carolyn, right now that is all I've got," Abigail said. "And frankly, that's more than I had before he arrived. So let's just take one day at a time - unless you want a piece of this fight?"

Before Carolyn could answer, Tyler came in from the kitchen and sat down at the table, "Rafford said to tell you goodnight. He went out to the barn."

Just after Tyler had gone upstairs to get ready for bed, Sheriff Coleman appeared at the front door.

"Good evening, Abigail. Sorry to stop by so late, but it's been one of those days," he said with a smile. "Carolyn, it's good to see you again."

"Curtis, you didn't drive all the way out here to welcome Carolyn home," Abigail said. "Is something wrong?"

"No, I don't think so," the Sheriff said tentatively. "It's just, well, did Rafford ever say anything to you about having a daughter?"

"No, he doesn't talk much about himself. He told me he was married once, but he never mentioned any children. Why?"

"Well, I told you I was doing some checking, just to be safe. I haven't found anything else about him, but in Saratoga Springs, I found a death certificate for a little girl, Cassandra Brown, who died a couple of years ago; she was only four years old. The girl's father was listed as Rafford Brown," the Sheriff paused to let it all sink in.

"How did the little girl die?" Carolyn asked.

"Asphyxiation was all it said on the certificate. I'm trying to find out more from the local authorities. He never mentioned anything?"

Abigail shook her head, "No, nothing."

"Were any charges filed?" Carolyn asked prompting a severe look from her mother.

"No charges, of any kind, have ever been filed against Rafford and, as far as I can tell, no charges were filed against anyone when the little girl died," Sheriff Coleman quickly answered. "I wasn't sure if I should even tell you about this, I really don't think it means anything. But I thought he might have said something to you that would explain it. I'll let you know if I find out anything."

After the Sheriff had left, Carolyn asked, "So, what do we do now?"

"Do? Nothing," Abigail said. "This doesn't change anything. The Sheriff is being overly protective, and so are you. Rafford Brown is a good and decent man."

"What if you are wrong? What if he's not the man that he seems to be?" Carolyn pushed.

"I trust him; even with my life," Abigail said firmly.

"And with Tyler's life, too?" Carolyn said and then bit her lip as soon as she had said it.

༁ྀ

Chapter Nineteen

Rafford awoke shortly after midnight, his heart racing and his breath coming in short gasps; fear and outright panic rolled over him. He sat up in bed, straining his eyes, peering through the darkness. Nothing. He switched on the battery-powered headlamp that he kept hanging by the bed and looked around the tack room. Still nothing; everything appeared to be just where it belonged. Why did he have this overwhelming sense of anxiety? Why did he feel as though something – something very important -- had suddenly changed?

He was accustomed to waking up in the middle of the night; it happened frequently following his recurring dream about Casey. On those occasions, as soon as he realized it was the dream, his composure returned and he would eventually go back to sleep. This night was different. He stoked the fire in the wood stove, adding another log and hoping to chase the chill he felt deep down in his bones. He took a long draw on the water bottle he kept by the bed, switched off the light and slipped back under the covers.

As he lay there, unable to sleep, he began to remember fragments of the dream that awakened him with such a feeling of dread and disaster. He only remembered bits and pieces, as if seen through shattered glass, but he knew it was not his usual dream. Hazy and muddled images gradually came to him; first images of Casey and then of Tyler, both weighing heavily on his heart. He felt a feeling of abject failure wash over him and he knew, somehow, that he had failed them both and let them down. He sensed that there was someone else in the dream, too, but he could not remember whom. A blurry image, rife with shadows, was the only vision that came back to him. This unknown person stood deep in the shadows, watching him, as though waiting for something to happen.

"It's only a dream," he said aloud.

It was not the dream that disturbed him, however. He had learned to accept the troubling dreams that visited so frequently. This night, however, he could not shake the uneasiness, the sense that something had changed and not for the better. He lay in the darkness and tried to clear his mind – hoping that the answer would come to him before he fell back to sleep.

Moonlight filtered through the worn window shade casting an eerie dim glow over the room. He closed his eyes and listened to the sounds of night in the mountains. He heard the trees stirring in the soft night breeze and the sound of coyotes wailing deep in the distant darkness. For nearly two years, he had gone to sleep listening to this Adirondack lullaby but tonight, for the first time, it brought no comfort. Tonight, he longed for something more. Tonight, he felt completely alone. He tossed and turned for a very long time, and then, just before dawn, sleep overtook him.

Rafford woke with Dog's wet nose nuzzling his face. The room was awash with sunlight, and in the bright light he saw Smokey sitting next to the wood stove and Tyler standing in the doorway, looking at him.

"Tyler," he said groggily, "what time is it?"

"Almost nine thirty," the boy answered. "Are you alright? I brought you some coffee."

Rafford sat up and took the coffee cup, "I'm fine. I didn't sleep much last night; I guess I made up for it this morning."

"I fed the chickens and put out some fresh water and hay, but the goats are not happy," Tyler said.

Rafford half groaned and half laughed, "They are never happy until the morning milking is done. Thanks for taking care of the other animals; I'll tend to the goats."

Tyler waited outside the tack room while Rafford dressed, then they walked together to the barn. Rafford drained the coffee cup, and handed it back to the boy.

Tyler stood watching him milk for a few minutes and then asked, "Can I take the dogsled out after lunch, today? The dogs are begging to run and I want to show my mom how I can handle the sled."

"I don't know, Tyler. I have a lot to do today, and this late start is going to put me way behind. After morning chores I've got to split and move firewood and then I have to go into Cold River to pick up the parts I ordered for the plow on the Kubota." Rafford saw the disappointment on the boy's face. "Are you ready to handle it alone?"

"Yes, sir!" the boy said excitedly. "I can do it. I won't bother you at all!"

Rafford smiled at him, "OK, then, but, you have to promise me that you will be very, very careful; no showing-off. Just take the dogs for a run around the property. Promise?"

"I promise!" Tyler said eagerly.

When Tyler had finished his lunch, he exchanged secret nods with his grandmother and then quietly slipped out to the barn. Rafford had skipped lunch and was splitting firewood behind the barn.

After Abigail and Carolyn had cleared the table, Abigail said, "Get your coat, dear, your son has something to show you."

The two women stood on the porch looking toward the barn where the sound of barking dogs rattled off every wall. A moment later, Smokey and Dog emerged pulling the dogsled with Tyler standing on the runners, smiling broadly. He turned the sled neatly in front of the porch and called the dogs to a halt.

Carolyn beamed at him, "Tyler, I am very impressed. You really do know how to run Grandpa's sled!"

"Isn't it beautiful, Mom -- see how the wood shines in the sun? Rafford and I put on two coats of varnish, to protect the wood, and I waxed the runners with ski wax, so they slide perfectly. I bet this is the fastest sled in the Adirondacks. Uncle Amos told me that Grandpa used to race it; and he won, too!"

"Well, I don't know about that," Carolyn said, with a glance toward Abigail, "but there will be no racing for you. Nice and easy does it, okay?"

"I know," the boy answered, "but someday, when I'm older..."

Abigail spoke up, "Tyler, why don't you show your Mother how well you handle the sled. Follow the practice track around the barnyard, just like you do with Uncle Amos."

Tyler nodded solemnly, adjusted his gloves, turned to the dogs and firmly called, "Hup!"

The dogs responded eagerly and they were off, running easily as Tyler guided the sled confidently through the first couple of turns. The dogs had settled into a comfortable trot by the time the sled disappeared behind the barn.

"He's very proud of himself," Abigail commented.

"I can tell," Carolyn answered, "but I wasn't prepared for how small he looks, behind Daddy's sled. He does seem to handle it well."

Both women watched intently as the sled reappeared between the livestock pen and the holding pond. Carolyn offered polite applause as Tyler neared the porch, but the boy did not seem to notice.

Abigail explained, "He's not done yet. There is a second part to his practice circuit."

Tyler leaned on the sled and called to the dogs again, as they neatly turned for the gap between the barn and the tack room. Then circling completely around the barn, they passed through the gap, again, and disappeared behind the tack room.

Abigail and Carolyn turned their eyes toward the livestock pen, looking for the sled to reappear, but it did not. They glanced at each other, for reassurance, and then back toward the pen, but still no sled.

Suddenly, they heard Tyler's voice cry clear and strong, "Rafford! Help! Help me!"

Everyone moved at once. Carolyn and Abigail ran from the porch toward the sound of Tyler's voice while Rafford came running from behind the barn. Rafford reached the pond first and found Tyler standing motionless next to the sled, in the middle of the iced-over pond. The two dogs were still harnessed to the sled, but Dog had fallen through the ice and was splashing noisily in the icy water. Smokey lay flat on the slick surface, his claws dug into the ice, trying to keep from being dragged into the water by Dog's thrashing about.

"Tyler!" Carolyn cried out when she saw his predicament.

"Mom! Dog is drowning – what do I do?" Tyler's voice cracked with fear.

Carolyn answered, "Don't worry about the dog – just turn around and get back here, where it's safe!"

"No!" Rafford shouted. "Tyler, don't move! The ice may break more – I will get you out of there."

Carolyn started to argue, but Abigail, wrapped her arms around her daughter and said, "Rafford knows what he is doing; give him a chance."

Rafford spoke again, but this time his voice was very calm and reassuring, "Tyler, please do exactly what I tell you.

Everything will be all right. First I want you to lie down on your stomach – but move very, very slowly."

The boy did as he was told. Rafford peeled off his heavy coat, and then began to crawl slowly out onto the ice.

"Rafford, wait!" Amos had suddenly appeared near the barn. He hurried toward the pond, dragging a wooden ladder behind him.

They slid the ladder onto the ice, and Rafford crawled forward pushing the ladder in front of him until the end of the ladder touched the soles of Tyler's boots.

"Okay, Tyler," Rafford said calmly, "the ladder is right behind you. I want you to slide backward, very slowly, until you are on top of the ladder. Then you can just shinny down the ladder to safety."

"But what about Dog and Smokey?" the boy said, his voice trembling.

"They'll be alright. Once you are safe, I will get them out," Rafford answered.

Abigail joined in, "Just do what Rafford says, Tyler. The dogs will be fine."

Tyler slid backwards climbing onto the ladder. Carolyn tried to call out to him to be careful, but could only coax a whimper from her voice. Abigail held her close and whispered to Amos that he should bring some blankets from the tack room.

When Tyler reached the bottom of the ladder, Rafford hugged him briefly, and then told him to crawl the rest of the way off the ice. A moment later, the boy was safe in his mother's arms.

Rafford pushed the ladder forward until it was alongside the sled and the end of the ladder extended slightly over the edge of the broken ice. Rafford inched his way along the ladder, until he reached the sled.

"Easy, Smokey," he said to the old dog as he reached for the rope harness. "Let's see if we can get you out of here."

First, he unclipped the section of the harness that connected Smokey and Dog. Then, he pulled out his Buck knife and cut through the harness that held Smokey to the sled. The dog was free, but he did not move.

"Tyler," Rafford shouted over his shoulder, "call Smokey; tell him to come to you."

Tyler wriggled free from Carolyn's embrace and clapped his hands twice as he called the dog. At first, Smokey seemed not to hear him, but then he turned his head, barked once, rose to all four feet and walked toward the boy.

"One down," Rafford said to himself and then turned his attention to Dog.

He slid further along the ladder toward the splashing dog, hoping he could pull him out by the harness, but knowing it would not be easy. As he eased out toward the last rung on the ladder, he heard the ice below him cracking and he knew that he could not wait. He called Dog's name loudly, and lunged for the harness. At the very moment that his fingers grasped the rope near the dog's neck, the ice gave way, and Rafford fell, head first into the icy water.

The pond was just deep enough that he could not reach bottom. Kicking his feet and swimming hard with his free hand, Rafford came up gasping for air. He heard someone calling his name, but the voice was fuzzy and seemed to come from very far away. Still clutching Dog's rope harness with one hand, he treaded water to stay afloat and grabbed the end of the ladder with his free hand. He tried to pull himself up onto the ice, but the ladder slid toward him, broke through the ice and slipped down into the water. Fortunately, the ladder was long enough to reach the bottom of the pond and it stood up straight, leaning against the ice.

Rafford quickly planted one foot on a rung of the ladder and, hoping the ice would hold, he climbed up, dragging Dog beside him. Finally, he was able to pull and then push the dog to safety on the surface of the frozen pond. Dog did not wait to be called; he gave one good shake to shed some of the frigid water and then sprinted for the shore.

Rafford climbed up one more rung on the ladder then eased his body flat onto the surface of the ice. He tried to pull the ladder up behind him, but he did not have the strength. He lay there, motionless trying to find the energy to move.

Amos called out, "Rafford, I'm going to throw you a rope. Get ready!"

Rafford picked up his head, looking toward the sound, but his eyes would not focus. Amos' aim was true and the last coil of the rope hit Rafford on the side of the head. He took the rope in his hand, coiling it around his wrist.

Amos started to pull on the other end, but Rafford called out, "No! Wait!"

He reached out, looped the rope around one of the sled runners, and then wrapped the rope around his wrist, again. Amos, Tyler, Abigail and Carolyn took hold of the other end of the rope and the four of them dragged Rafford and the sled safely to the edge of the pond.

Rafford shivered uncontrollably as Amos covered him with blankets. He struggled to breathe, his breath coming only in small gulps, as he they surrounded him in the snow.

"We should take him to the tack room; the wood stove will warm him up," Tyler said.

"Good idea, Tyler," Abigail replied. "Why don't you run ahead and stoke the fire?"

Tyler was off on the run with Carolyn following close behind. Amos helped Rafford to his feet and, with Abigail supporting his other side, they half-carried, half-dragged him, stumbling through the deep snow toward the tack room. Rafford tried to walk, but the most he could do was shuffle his feet slowly forward.

Tyler met them at the tack room door. They sat Rafford on the room's lone chair next to the wood stove.

"I found some warm clothes for him," Tyler said. "Uncle Amos and I can help him change."

Abigail and Carolyn took the hint and stepped outside. Before long, Rafford was sitting by the stove in dry clothes sipping Abigail's chamomile tea with honey. Gradually the shivering stopped and he began to breathe normally again.

"Are you feeling better, Rafford?" Tyler asked.

Rafford tried to smile at him, "A lot better. I don't think I have ever been that cold, in my life. Are you okay?"

The boy nodded, "I'm okay. Rafford, I'm sorry. I don't know what happened, it was so fast. The sled started to slide and I couldn't stop, or turn, or anything. Then we were on the ice and I heard it crack; that's when I yelled for you. I'm really sorry."

"It's alright, Tyler," Rafford said as he put his arm around the boy. "Accidents happen. I'm just glad everyone is okay."

"Thanks to you, Rafford," Abigail's voice cracked with emotion as she spoke. "Now, drink your tea."

Amos tousled Tyler's hair, "Tyler, you surprised me! You knew all the right things to do to help make Rafford feel better. How did you know that? Are you a boy scout, or something?"

Tyler answered without looking him in the eye, "Rafford taught me, a couple of weeks ago. I just remembered what he said to do."

Carolyn stood alone, in a corner of the room, far from the others. She had not said one word since Tyler crawled off the ice. Now she stood watching from a distance, absent-mindedly chewing on her lower lip. At last, she took a deep breath and walked over to where the others clustered around Rafford.

"Tyler, why don't you go back to the house and change your clothes? I'll be there in a minute. I want to speak with Rafford."

Carolyn waited for the boy to leave the room, and then continued, "Rafford, thank you for helping Ty, but I hope you understand, now, why I worry about him. I mean, he is still just a boy, and all this dog-sledding, snowshoeing, tractor driving is just too much – too dangerous – for him."

Rafford turned to look at her and said evenly, "The boy didn't do anything wrong. It was an accident; it could have happened to Amos, to me, to anyone. Don't blame him; if you want to blame somebody, blame me."

"You see? That attitude is why Tyler ended up out there on the ice today. Blame you? Yes, I do blame you!" she shouted as tears filled her eyes. "Ever since we got here, you have been encouraging him to do things that just aren't safe! Tyler is my son, not yours, and I won't let you put him in danger. He could have been killed out there today! Maybe that doesn't mean much to you – you already lost a daughter – but I am not going to lose Tyler!"

"That is enough!" Abigail shouted at her daughter. "This man risked his own life for your son and you treat him like this? You should be ashamed of yourself!"

Abigail's admonition went unheard, as Carolyn had already run through the open door headed toward the house. Rafford did not hear Abigail, either. He was doubly stung by Carolyn's tirade and by what she said about his daughter.

"Rafford, I'm so sorry," Abigail said. "Sometimes, Carolyn – "

"Abigail, don't," Rafford interrupted. "She's right. She is Tyler's mother and that makes her right."

He paused for several seconds, the said, "How did she know about my daughter?"

Abigail sighed deeply, "I should have told you. Sheriff Coleman has been checking up on you. He told us, last night, that he found a death certificate for a little girl that he thought might be your daughter."

"He was right," Rafford said softly and looked away from her. "I'm really tired. Would you two leave me alone for a while? I need to rest."

"I'll put the sled away before I go," Amos offered but Rafford just stared, blankly, at the fire.

Abigail found Carolyn sitting on the couch in the living room, her legs pulled up against her chest. Her eyes were red and tears glistened on her cheeks.

"Where is Tyler?" Abigail asked softly.

"Upstairs," Carolyn answered as Abigail sat down on the end of the sofa nearest to her. "Mother, don't start, please. I know I was wrong. Why do I do it? Why do I get so upset that I do things and say things like that?"

"I don't know, honey, "Abigail said as she stroked Carolyn's head. "I know you have a good heart, but sometimes you get so angry! It's hard raising a child on your own, and Carolyn, you have done a great job with Tyler. But you need to ease up a little. Enjoy being his mother, enjoy watching him grow-up and be grateful when someone like Rafford comes along to help."

Carolyn sobbed as fresh tears rolled down her cheeks, "Why am I always so mean to him? Since that very first day, I've never missed a single opportunity to put him down. Is it because he can do things for Tyler that I can't do? "

Carolyn cried still harder.

Finally, she spoke again, "Did you notice? Did you notice who Tyler called for when he was in trouble? Not Mom, no – he called for Rafford! And he was right; Rafford was right there to help him! Oh God, I can't believe I said that about his little girl!" her voice dissolved into more sobs.

"What did you say about his little girl?" Tyler said as he charged down the stairs. "What did you say about Casey?"

Abigail spoke to him first, "You know about his daughter?"

Tyler nodded, but kept looking at his mother waiting for her to answer him. When she didn't answer, he asked again, "What is going on? Why are you crying and what does it have to do with Casey?"

"Cassandra, his daughter's name was Cassandra and she..." Carolyn could not say the word.

"She died," Tyler said. "Rafford told me all about her; he carries a picture of her in his Bible."

"Tyler, did Rafford tell you what happened; how she died?" Abigail asked tentatively.

"She drowned," Tyler said.

Carolyn groaned and her sobs started again.

Tyler continued, "Rafford wasn't home when it happened. Casey fell into a neighbor's swimming pool and drowned. He feels bad because he thinks he should have been there to protect her."

Abigail held out her arms to Tyler and he came to her. They embraced and Abigail whispered to him, "I love you, Tyler. Your Mom loves you, too, and right now she really needs a hug."

Tyler walked slowly to his mother, leaned toward her and wrapped his arms around her neck. Carolyn pulled him tight against her, buried her face in his shoulder and wept.

಄ ಄

Chapter Twenty

Rafford spent another restless night, haunted not by dreams this time, but by indecision. He closed his eyes but could not sleep. When he rose with the sun on the day before Christmas, he finally knew what it was that he had to do.

He took his backpack from the wall and filled it with his clothes and his few meager belongings, then placed Casey's picture safely on top of the pile. He downed a mug of stale coffee from the pot on the wood stove and then set about his daily routine. The frigid morning air clawed at his cheeks and his breath hung in great white clouds about his head. It would be two or three hours before the winter sun would warm the day, but he could not wait – he had much to do. He worked steadily, but with a renewed sense of purpose. Mid-morning, Abigail walked into the barn and found him mucking out the stalls.

"Good morning. We missed you at breakfast. I thought you might be hungry," she said, raising the bucket in her hand.

"Abigail, food is not the answer to all the world's problems," Rafford said with a smile as he took the pail from her. "But, I will admit, that your cooking does make me forget about those problems for a while."

They sat, side-by-side, on hay bales while he ate. An uncomfortable silence sat between them, waiting to be broken.

"Tyler wanted to bring the pail, but I had to talk to you alone, Rafford. I don't know why I always end up apologizing for my daughter, but here I am again, and truth be told, I need to apologize for myself, too. I should have told Curtis Coleman to put his investigation where the sun won't shine, but I didn't."

Rafford shook his head, "He was just looking out for you, Abigail. He did what he thought he had to do to protect you."

"But it was wrong, Rafford," Abigail protested. "After all you have done for me – why, if not for you, I'd be lying next to Roger in the cold hard ground. I don't need any investigating by Curtis to protect me. Then, when he told me about your daughter, I should have come to you right away, as a friend, and as another parent who knows how it feels to lose a child. I'm so sorry, Rafford."

She paused, dabbed at the corners of her eyes with a tissue, and then continued, "I guess I thought everything would be okay, if I left things unsaid. Then yesterday, everything happened so fast, and Carolyn – I had no idea she would say what she said. There is no excuse for her behavior; if it helps, she feels terrible about what she said to you."

"But, Abigail, she's right," Rafford said quietly.

"No! She is not right," Abigail interrupted. "Blaming you for what happened, or what might have happened, to Tyler is crazy."

"She is his mother, Abigail, She will always be his mother, and me – I'm just some guy passing through. She can't let someone like me get between her and her son. I didn't mean to, but I got caught up in my own feelings. I was pretending – selfishly pretending – that I was part of a family, again."

Rafford was quiet for some time, and then he said, "After that first night, you never again asked me why I had been living in a tent for two years."

"You are entitled to your privacy," Abigail answered with a smile. "Besides, as I came to know you better, knowing what had happened before you came here didn't seem as important."

Rafford took a deep breath, and then exhaled with a sigh, "That is very generous of you, but now I think it is important for you to know and, hopefully, to understand.

When Casey died, my whole world fell apart. She drowned in a neighbor's swimming pool.   I wasn't home when it happened; I was out of town on business. She was my little girl. I should have been there to keep her safe. I blamed myself for what happened and my wife blamed me, too. I know, now, that she simply could not cope with her grief and her anger at losing her daughter, but back then my guilt and her rage tore our marriage apart. The day we buried Casey my wife walked away and never came back.

I didn't know what to do. I couldn't sleep. I couldn't eat. I stopped going to work. I was an environmental scientist, doing the work that I had dreamed about doing ever since I was a kid, but it suddenly meant nothing to me. They offered me a leave of absence but I didn't even bother to sign the papers. Within a month after Casey died, my wife, my job, everything was gone. I was totally alone and living in an empty house surrounded by the deepest, darkest, sadness I could ever have imagined. Every morning I awoke wondering how I would get through another day. Every evening I sat in the shadows with a pistol in my hand, praying for the strength to pull the trigger.

The Adirondacks saved me. One day in sheer desperation, I packed my camping gear, drove to Old Forge, put my canoe in the water and paddled away. I didn't know where I was going, or what I was going to do, but I was determined to find some answers in the mountains. If not, I was ready use the pistol that I carried in my backpack to put an end to my misery. I was running away but, thank God, I ran to the one place that had always been a touchstone for me; the one place where I felt I really belonged.

I know it sounds trite, but the mountains became my sanctuary. Each day I paddled like a maniac from dawn to dusk. I did every portage I could find, the tougher the better, torturing my body. At night I collapsed, exhausted, into deep dreamless sleep. Apparently, it was the right tonic, because I gradually began to feel I could make it through. Three weeks after leaving Old Forge, I returned. I sold my truck to the first buyer I could find, restocked my supplies and headed back into the mountains. There I stayed, until I found my way to your front door.

The thing is, now I can't go back. Two years of hiding from the rest of the world and running away from my own demons is enough. You showed me what was missing in my life and reminded me about what is really important. You welcomed me into your family. These weeks with you and with Tyler have made me long for a home and a family again. This is your home, your family – and I need to find my own. So, I'm stuck – I can't go back to hiding in the mountains, but I can't stay here, either. There's only one choice left."

Abigail looked at him and, without blinking, said, "This could be your home, too."

He smiled, "Why, Mrs. Sherwood, are you proposing to me?"

Abigail laughed, "No, I need a more mature man. I could adopt you!"

They laughed and embraced and while still holding him tightly, Abigail whispered, "Thank you, Rafford. I will miss you, terribly. I wish you would at least stay for Christmas – Tyler will miss you so; me too."

When Abigail released her embrace, Rafford said, "I thought about Christmas, but I think I should go today. Amos is going to visit his daughter for the holidays. I imagine I can stay at his place while he's away. Tyler can handle the animals but he will need a hand milking the goats. I won't be far away, so if there's a big snow I'll come over and run the Kubota for you."

"Thank you. I expect, we'll get by, at least until Carolyn and Tyler leave for Texas. After that, we'll just have to see what happens. Will you be with us for lunch?"

"I'll try. I have to go into town to pick up that new starter for the tractor. I'll definitely stop in to say goodbye."

The rest of the day passed by in a blur of activity. It was nearly four o'clock when Rafford walked into the kitchen and found Carolyn taking gingerbread from the oven. He was sure that she heard him come in, but she did not look up until she had moved each of cookies from the cookie sheet onto the cooling rack.

Rafford spoke, "You must have special influence here; I've never seen Abigail let anyone else cook in her kitchen."

"Well, she has to tolerate me, since we're related," Carolyn forced a smile. She paused before continuing, "You on the other hand, don't have to tolerate me. In fact, you have every right to think the worst of me. I have been cruel and hurtful and completely unfair to you since the very first time we met. And what have you done, in return? You've cared for my mother, befriended my son, and even risked your own life to keep him safe. You don't make it easy for a girl to dislike you. Rafford, 'I'm sorry' just isn't enough, but it's all I've got. I am sorry and I hope that someday you will forgive me."

"That's very kind of you, Carolyn. There's some truth in what you just said, but there is also some truth in what you said yesterday. I selfishly took advantage of your mother's kindness and your son's friendship. I got carried away and forgot that just living somewhere doesn't make it your home. I acted as if this wonderful place was my home and your family was my own. I overstepped my bounds and for that I owe you an apology."

They were both silent for a moment then Carolyn said softly, "Mother says you are leaving. I wish you would reconsider. We will all miss you and, if Tyler and I go to Texas, I don't know how my mother will get by all alone."

"If you go to Texas?" Rafford asked. "I thought you had decided to go."

"Did I say 'if'?" Carolyn sounded flustered. "I meant, well, I think we should go but Tyler wants no part of it."

Rafford nodded, "He told me. It will be a big change from Boston. I imagine it is hard for him to leave his school, his friends."

"I don't know what he told you but he doesn't want to live in Boston, either," she said. "He wants to stay here!"

His surprise showed on Rafford's face but, before he could respond, they heard the rumble of Amos' truck rolling up the gravel drive into the barnyard.

Abigail came into the kitchen, with Tyler close by her side. The boy's eyes were red and swollen.

"Amos is here. I explained to Tyler that you were going to stay at Amos' place for a while. I also told him that you would come back to visit before he leaves for Texas."

Rafford forced a smile, "Of course, I'll be back to visit. Tyler, if those goats give you any trouble, you call me – okay?"

Tyler nodded and turned his face away, clutching his grandmother's arm.

"Amos is waiting for me. He's driving to Burlington tomorrow, so we better go," Rafford said.

He walked over to Abigail, embraced her and rested his hand on Tyler's shoulder, "Thank you, for everything, Abigail. I will miss you, all. Merry Christmas."

On the drive from Deer Run to Cold River, Rafford kept silent and Amos wisely did not to try to force a conversation. Amos turned the truck into Lou's Country Corner as the sun dropped behind the mountains.

"I never pass by here, without picking up a couple of Lou's blueberry muffins. You want me to get you anything?"

Rafford shook his head no.

As Amos entered the store, Rafford saw Joanne Farber, Abigail's pastor, coming out. She and Amos exchanged a few words and then she came toward the truck. Rafford turned away and pulled his hat lower on his forehead.

"Rafford – Merry Christmas!" she called,

Rafford rolled down the window and forced a smile, "Merry Christmas, Pastor Joanne."

"Amos tells me you won't be coming to church tonight with Abigail and the family. You'll be sorry – our Christmas Eve service is not to be missed. The children's pageant is unpredictable but always a blessing. You really should try to come."

"I guess Amos didn't tell you, I'm not staying at Deer Run anymore," Rafford said trying not to let his voice betray his emotions.

"No, he didn't say anything about that. When did all of this happen?

"I've been thinking about it ever since Carolyn came back from Texas," he lied. "Anyway, thanks for the invitation."

"Rafford I know Carolyn can be difficult, but –"

"No – it's not her fault. I just don't want to overstay my welcome. Knowing when to leave is important."

Pastor Joanne studied him for a moment then said, "I'm sorry you won't be at Deer Run any longer. You were a great help to Abigail and what you did for Tyler was amazing. But if you stay in the area, I hope you will come to church when you can."

She began to walk away, then stopped and turned back and said, "Sometimes knowing when to stay is even harder than knowing when to leave. Sometimes you just have to hang on to what really matters. If you change your mind, Christmas Eve service starts at seven. You will be in my prayers, Rafford."

For supper, Rafford made cornbread to go with Amos' venison stew and the two men ate mostly in silence. After dinner, Amos tried to interest Rafford in a game of gin rummy, but Rafford declined. Instead, they sat listening to an old Christmas concert being rebroadcast on the Saranac Lake radio station.

At about nine o'clock, Rafford went to his room and was getting ready for bed when he heard the phone ring. He could not hear what Amos was saying, but his voice sounded agitated. As Rafford opened the door and heard Amos calling for him.

"Rafford!" Amos shouted, "We gotta go!"

Before Rafford could answer, Amos came running down the hall, "That was Abigail – our boy is gone! Tyler's gone!"

"What happened?"

"She said she will tell us when we get there – right now, we gotta move!"

Amos pushed the old truck for every ounce of speed he could on the way back to Deer Run. Roaring through the darkness he nearly missed the turn for Abigail's driveway. As they approached the house, they saw Abigail standing under the porch light in the open doorway. Rafford jumped out of the truck and right away heard the sound of snowmobiles on the mountain and his heart sank.

He ran up the porch steps, "Abigail, what happened? Where is Tyler?"

Abigail's hands were trembling when she took his arm, "He's gone. We came home from Christmas Eve services and he went up to his room. A few minutes later Carolyn and I heard the snowmobiles up on the mountain and stepped out here on the porch for a look. I was surprised when Tyler didn't come down, so I went to check on him. He wasn't in his room, but when I looked out his window, I saw him racing toward the mountain on the dogsled. That's when I called you."

Carolyn burst through the door, bumping into Rafford. "Did Mom tell you? He took the dogsled and he's gone up there," she looked fearfully toward the mountain. "Rafford, we heard gunshots! I'm going after him."

"No, Carolyn," Abigail implored, "you can't go up there in the dark."

Rafford quickly added, "You should stay here, in case he comes back. Besides I can move faster without you."

Amos tossed Rafford the keys to his truck, "Drive part way, you'll save some time!"

As Rafford backed the truck away from the house, he heard Abigail calling, "Wait! Rafford, wait!"

She ran up to the side of the truck and pushed a rifle and a box of shells under Rafford's backpack in the truck bed.

"Just in case," she said.

Rafford nodded grimly, "You better call Sheriff Coleman – just in case."

Rafford sped along the dirt road, his mind racing. All he could think about was Tyler somewhere out there in the dark. If anything happened to him. He could not finish that thought. The old truck bounced hard and then slid through a set of ice-covered ruts at the end of the road. When he hit the brakes the wheels locked-up and the truck skidded forward landing with a soft thump in the huge pile of snow at the end of the road.

He quickly strapped on his snowshoes and daypack. He picked up the rifle, hesitated only a moment, and then filled his jacket pocket with shells.   Rifle in hand, he set off along the usual trail at a half trot.

A full moon lit up the night sky and reflected off the snow casting long eerie shadows. Once his eyes adjusted to the moonlight, he quickly spotted fresh dogsled tracks, just where he had expected to find them. The cold chafed against his face as he pressed forward. The temperature was dropping fast now that the sun had gone down. He wondered if Tyler had dressed warm enough for the cold. Pushing steadily onward, he scrambled over a downed tree and then clearly heard three gunshots not far ahead. He stopped and listened but all he could hear was the angry growl and whine of snowmobile engines.

He knew he was close, but he was not sure just how close. Then, ahead in the shadows, he saw the dogsled. The two dogs were huddled together, tied to a tree. He saw no sign of Tyler. Rafford crept closer and peered through the tree branches.

The headlights of four snowmobiles lit up the scene before him but he still took a moment to comprehend what he saw. George Harder stood, silhouetted by one headlight, gesturing with his rifle to the three other men. Rafford squinted his eyes against the glare of the lights searching for some sign of Tyler. Off to one side, he saw a man crouched in the snow, bending over the lifeless body of a deer. The man was trussing her hind-legs with hands covered in blood. Rafford's eyes scanned quickly across to the other side of the clearing where he spotted Tyler kneeling in the snow, not far from where George Harder now stood. Tyler was holding the fawn in his arms. Rafford saw Harder signal to two other men who began to walk toward Tyler. He could not see the boy's face but knew that he had to be terrified.

Rafford stood up and walked directly into the light, the rifle resting in the crook of his arm. He walked straight toward Harder until he stood between him and the boy.

"That's close enough," Harder said, leveling his rifle at Rafford. "Well, well, Mr. Brown; it seems as if everyone wants to join our little Christmas Eve party."

"It's nice to know you're in the holiday spirit, Harder," Rafford tried to keep his voice calm and in control, even though his heart was pounding, "but trespassing, hunting deer out of season, and pointing guns at little boys – I don't seem to remember any of those as being Christmas traditions."

"Why, Brown, what can you be talking about," Harder said, sarcastically.

Rafford noticed movement out of the corner of his eye, but before he could react the man who had been trussing the doe, slipped up behind him and punched him hard in the kidney. Rafford fell to the ground as the man ripped the rifle from his grasp. He landed on his hands and knees, looking up at Harder's sneering face.

"Brown, you have been nothing but trouble since you showed up here," Harder said. "No, trouble is too strong a word; irritation is more like it. Like one of those pesky deer flies that just won't go away. But, tonight you are terribly confused. Why, we were out for a peaceful ride in the woods when we came upon this poor doe, freshly killed by your rifle."

Harder nodded to the man holding Rafford's rifle. The man raised the gun, pointed it at the dead deer and pulled the trigger. The gun only made a soft clicking sound.

"Not even loaded! What did you think you were going to do with an unloaded rifle?" Harder shook his head and snickered.

A single gunshot exploded, and Rafford snapped his head around toward the sound. The man holding his rifle stood over the doe, as smoke curled from the barrel.

"After you shot this poor deer, and realized that we had seen everything, why you even took a shot at us, hitting one of our snowmobiles," Harder nodded again at the man with Rafford's rifle.

Again, he fired and this time the bullet struck the windscreen of the closest snowmobile. The man worked the lever action again, to be sure it was empty and then put it down next to Rafford.

"Fortunately, you were overcome by our numbers, and we were able to subdue you, before any more damage was done."

"Just who do you think is going to believe this little fairy tale, Harder," Rafford said.

"Oh, I can be very persuasive. Besides, do you really think anyone will listen to a drifter and a little boy," Harder laughed. "Oh, I think they will find it very easy to believe our story."

"Come on, George," one of the other men said, "Let's get out of here."

"Patience, we'll go as soon as Andy gets back," Harder said, and then hearing a snowmobile approaching, he added, "Here he comes now."

The snowmobile pulled up in the shadows and parked behind the others. Two men got off and walked toward Harder prompting Rafford to smile broadly when he saw who they were.

"Sheriff Coleman and Ranger Warner," the quaver in Harder's voice betrayed his surprise, "we didn't expect to see you out here on Christmas Eve."

Warner walked directly over to Rafford and stood with him and Tyler, "Are you two OK?" Rafford and Tyler each nodded in reply.

"Put the gun down, Harder," Coleman said, his hand resting on the butt of the pistol strapped to his side.

Harder feigned surprise, "What? Oh, this looks worse than it is, Sheriff, but I am glad you're here! It seems Mr. Brown has been jacklighting deer; he shot that poor doe over there, and even took a shot at us when we caught him. It turns out she had a fawn – imagine that, Ranger, a fawn this time of year!"

"That is hard to believe," Warner answered.

"Well, there's the living proof right there," Harder pointed at the fawn, still held tight in Tyler's arms.

"I didn't mean the part about the fawn, Harder," Warner said mockingly, "I meant the rest of that hogwash you're dishing out! Rafford Brown would never jacklight deer, especially that deer; and if he took a shot at you, my guess is that you wouldn't be standing here to talk about it."

"Maybe, you want to rethink that story, Harder?" Sheriff Coleman offered.

"It happened just like I said, Sheriff, and the boys, here, will back me up, one hundred percent," Harder declared.

"Well, Ranger Warner," Coleman said, "it seems we have a difference of opinion, here. Perhaps you could shed a little light on the subject?"

"Thank you, Sheriff, I'd be glad to," Warner smirked as he pulled out his oversized flashlight. "Harder, you are right about one thing, a winter fawn is very unusual; in fact, it's so unusual that environmental scientists, like me, are interested in studying the phenomenon. So, when Rafford and Tyler told me about this pregnant doe, I decided to do some scientific observation. But, alas, a Ranger's life is a busy one and I just didn't have the time to sit in a tree stand out here, day after day, observing. So I did the next best thing."

Warner turned on the flashlight and pointed it high up in a fir tree on the edge of the clearing. The beam from his light reflected off something metallic, camouflaged among the branches.

"That, gentlemen, is an environmental scientist's best friend," Warner was clearly enjoying himself, now. "That is a motion activated video camera, with a very sensitive eye for use in low-light situations. If you will follow the beam of my flashlight, you will see that I have installed another motion-activated camera over here and yet another, over here."

They all followed his light as it pointed out the three cameras. Warner switched off the light and resumed his explanation.

"These cameras are incredibly sensitive, the least amount of motion activates them and they need very little light. Moonlight like this, is just as good as midday sun. The remarkable thing is that they are solar powered so –"

"Warner!" the sheriff interrupted, "its cold out here, and I would like to get home in time to see my kids open their gifts!"

"Sorry, Curtis," Warner replied. "So, the cameras turn on automatically when motion is detected, and the images are transmitted back to a digital recorder at my cabin. I have hours and hours of video of this winter fawn, including the lengthy segment shot here tonight, featuring every one of you, which prompted me to call Curtis a little while ago. So, Sheriff Coleman, you have all the evidence you could ever need for a long list of charges: trespassing, menacing, making a false police report, operating a snowmobile in a restricted area and taking a deer on state land out of season, just to get started."

"Wait a minute," Harder said, "I know when I'm getting railroaded. Trespassing, OK, but menacing? Get serious. As far as the other 'charges', about restricted areas and state land, Ranger you need to check your map."

"Oh, but I have, George," Warner retorted. "I pinpointed this location with GPS to validate my research and it seems that the published maps have perpetuated an erroneous state land boundary line. You are, without question, standing on land owned by the great state of New York. Rafford, please give my apologies to Mrs. Sherwood, but we are going to have to redo those boundary markers."

"Harder, you and your friends are in some deep trouble," Sheriff Coleman said in his most authoritative voice. "Being Christmas Eve, I have better things to do than take you into custody. But, at nine a.m. on December 26th, I expect all of you, to surrender yourselves at Town Hall. Don't make me come looking for you! Now, get on out of here."

When Harder and the others had gone, the three men gathered around Tyler. The boy still held the fawn, cradled in his arms.

Warner knelt down next to him, "Tyler that fawn won't make it out here without his mother. Can you take him back to Deer Run and look after him for a few days? He can do pretty well on goat's milk, at least for a while."

"Yes sir, I'll take care of him, I promise," Tyler said.

Rafford shook hands with the Sheriff and then with Warner, "Thank you. Talk about the cavalry riding to the rescue; you two really saved the day."

Warner and Sheriff Coleman drove off on the snowmobile while Rafford and Tyler walked back to the dogsled. Rafford had so much he wanted to say to him. So many promises that he had made to himself as he raced through the dark terrified that he would not find the boy in time. He wanted to say that he would be there to help with the fawn. He wanted to say that he would never be far away, again, that somehow, someway, he would always be there to keep him safe. He had so much he wanted to say, but the words lodged in his throat, jammed so tight he could barely breathe.

Tyler looked up at him and Rafford forced a smile to his lips. The boy held tight to the fawn and leaned up against Rafford and buried his face in Rafford's chest.

Rafford hesitated, at first, then put his arms around the boy, reassuringly. They held the embrace for several seconds, until the fawn started to squirm between them, then he said, quietly, "Tyler, let's go home."

Rafford draped the fawn across his shoulders. Tyler turned the dogsled around and, without a word, they started the long walk back to Deer Run.

When they neared the barnyard, Smokey and Dog strained at the harness, barking and yipping. Tyler fought to hold them back until he saw the porch light in the distance and then, with a nod of approval from Rafford, he let the dogs sprint the final stretch.

Abigail and Carolyn ran to meet them and together they wrapped Tyler in one joyous embrace. Carolyn tried to speak, but only managed to say his name over and over again through her tears.

Amos greeted Rafford, "Well, I'll be, an honest-to-God winter fawn, and on Christmas Eve, too!" Amos scratched the tiny deer behind the ears, and whispered to Rafford, "Everything go OK up there?"

Rafford nodded, "Everything went okay, thanks to Sheriff Coleman and Travis Warner. Oh, everything except your truck – I left it in a snow bank."

"That's alright, trucks don't matter; but little boys and good friends are priceless," Amos laughed as he put his arm around Rafford's shoulders.

Rafford heard Tyler say to his grandmother, "I promised to take care of him. Ranger Warner said he will like goat's milk."

"Oh, yes, goat's milk will be good," Abigail replied. "Did I ever tell you about the fawn that your Grandpa Roger and I raised, right here at Deer Run? Why, that was how this place got its name."

Chapter Twenty One

R afford and Tyler made a place in the barn for the fawn to sleep. They covered the stall floor with a thick layer of hay and the fawn quickly curled up in one corner.

Rafford said, "He did well with the goat's milk tonight. He seemed to know that you and your Grandmother would take care of him."

Tyler nodded his agreement, but never took his eyes off the tiny deer. "Do you think he misses his mother?" the boy asked.

"I don't know, Tyler. Sometimes animals just seem to understand about these things." He paused a long moment, then asked, "Did you see those men shoot her?"

Tyler nodded his head slowly up and down, "I was hiding behind a tree, watching. The doe just stood there, in the bright light, like she was a statue. The fawn was hiding behind her and then all of a sudden they shot her. The fawn was so scared he jumped up in the air and then he started running around. The men were chasing him but he was too quick. Finally, I just ran out in the middle of them and the fawn came running, straight to me."

"That was a very brave thing to do, Tyler," Rafford whispered.

"I was scared, but I couldn't let them shoot him, too. I didn't know what to do, and then I remembered how you said to trust myself. You said that sometimes it's not easy to know what to do, but that if I trusted myself, then I would always find the right answer."

Rafford put his arm around Tyler's shoulders and smiled at the boy.

Carolyn stood in the shadows by the barn door listening to every word. She cupped both hands over her mouth to silence the moan she felt welling up from deep inside her. Silently she slipped back outside brushing the tears from her eyes.

Later that night Rafford stood alone in the barnyard staring up at the stars. He heard footsteps behind him and turned to find Carolyn walking toward him.

"The night sky is more beautiful here, than anywhere," she said.

Rafford nodded agreement, "It's as if the mountains are wrapped in a blanket of stars."

"Rafford, I'm glad you have decided to stay," Carolyn said tentatively.

"How could I leave?" Rafford answered.

Carolyn nodded her understanding, "We're staying, too. Tyler didn't want to go to Texas, anyway, and now with a fawn to care for, well, I know when I'm outnumbered."

"It's really not a bad place, once you get used to it," he said with a smile.

Carolyn smiled back at him, "Yeah, I know, or at least, I used to know. I had forgotten how much I loved it here. Boston never felt like this – no matter how hard I tried – it never really felt like home. Tyler and I were together, but something was missing. I always told myself that this was my parent's home and that I had to make my own home, somewhere else. Boston is a great city, and so is Austin, but this is home. This is the only place where I have ever truly felt that I belonged. I lost that, once; I won't lose it again. After tonight, I don't think that Tyler will ever let it go."

She paused for a moment, as though thinking about something. "You should have seen him in church tonight. Pastor Joanne always includes every child in the Christmas pageant. They don't rehearse or anything, but the children seem to know what to do. Everyone gets a role and a costume when they arrive at church.

During the service, Pastor Joanne tells the Christmas story and the children help act it out. Anyway, Tyler was asked to be one of the shepherds tonight. Pastor Joanne's two Corgi dogs were dressed up as the sheep. Some of the other kids were wired – excited about Christmas and maybe they had a few too many Christmas cookies, you know? But not Tyler; he was so calm, so mature, and he took such good care of those dogs. Even when the other shepherds got a little crazy, those two 'sheep' stuck to Tyler like he really was their shepherd."

"He has a gift with animals, Carolyn, and he belongs here just as much as that little fawn belongs here. The Adirondacks are a special place and to be here, to discover who you are as a part of all this, is a true gift. Some of us just know it naturally while others of us will take a lifetime to learn it and make it our own. Tyler was given that gift – he got it from you and Abigail and Roger and whoever came before them. He's only a boy, but he has found himself here and if he remembers that one thing about himself, everything else will be fine." Rafford lowered his eyes and his voice, then continued, "I'm sorry – you don't need me to tell you about your own son."

Carolyn smiled at him warmly "Don't apologize. I might not have come to understand any of this if not for Tyler and if not for you, Rafford. You're right, Tyler belongs here – and you do, too. I don't understand it all but, somehow, this place is meant to be your home, too."

They stood together in silence for a few moments, and then Carolyn said, "Well, I had better go check on Tyler. He was so excited about the fawn; he may never get to sleep tonight."

She started walking back toward the house when Rafford said, "Carolyn – you're going the wrong direction. Tyler is in the barn."

She found him in the stall with the fawn. Tyler lay sleeping in the hay, covered with a blanket that she remembered seeing earlier on Rafford's bunk in the tack room. The fawn was curled up next to him, and Dog and Smokey both slept huddled at his feet. She stood perfectly still, burning this unforgettable picture in her memory. Then quietly she left the barn.

Carolyn walked over to where Rafford stood, still gazing at the stars. She moved close to him and, without saying a word, she took his hand in hers, as though it was the most natural thing she had ever done.

"Merry Christmas," she whispered and then she sighed deeply when he did not pull his hand away.

ABOUT THE AUTHOR

William Delia is an accomplished writer, songwriter and public speaker. Born in Connecticut and educated in California, he enjoyed a lengthy career as a non-profit executive and in the ministry. He has composed more than one hundred songs, both lyrics and music, and is the author of two completed novels, *Home to the Mountains* and *Healing River.*

He lives and writes in the foothills of the Adirondack Mountains of upstate New York. For more information see www.wmdeliabooks.com.

Made in the USA
Middletown, DE
12 November 2016